Pacesetters

The Black Temple

Mohmed Tukur Garba

MACMILLAN

First published 1981
Reprinted 1982, 1983

Published by
Macmillan Education
London and Basingstoke
*Companies and representatives in Lagos, Zaria, Manzini,
Nairobi, Singapore, Hong Kong, Delhi, Dublin, Auckland,
Melbourne, Tokyo, New York, Washington, Dallas.*

ISBN 0 333 31147 7 (Paper)
ISBN 0 333 33507 4 (Cased)

Printed in Hong Kong

Macmillan *Pacesetters*

All the novels in the Macmillan *Pacesetters* series deal with contemporary issues and problems in a way that is particularly designed to interest young adults, although the stories are such that they will appeal to all ages.

Chapter 1

As the Chief of Kofir stared hard at the picture in the evening newspaper, his expression began to change. First he thrust his head forward a little and his eyes narrowed, giving his face a new, hard, more mature look. His face contorted as if with rage and he pursed his lips as if whistling softly.

The officials who sat around him remained silent. They were curious but too afraid to say anything. They didn't know what was the matter with their Chief. As far as they were concerned, they themselves could be the main cause of his present change of mood. Some considered possibilities in their minds, cases in which they had done wrong and had gone away unpunished. What about the recent tax scandal....

The Chief muttered an abusive word and spat. Then he turned his gaze to the photograph again. It was the picture of a pregnant woman lying dead in a pool of blood. The woman had been so severely beaten that her head had swollen and was so unrecognisable that a person couldn't tell at a glance what it was. One eyeball—the right one—had been dug out of its socket.

Hurriedly, as if he thought someone was going to take the paper away, the Chief read the comment by the picture.

'Pictured left is the body of a pregnant dead woman caught within the grips of a Benin-based secret society. Secret societies take many forms—some are political associations, some are illegal business associations, and some are quite violent and murderous in executing their activities. The Federal Military Government has recently banned all civil servants from holding memberships in any secret society. It is our view and suggestion that the restriction on civil servants should be widened to include all citizens of this country.'

The Chief agreed with the suggestion. He felt it was the only way of containing the murderous activities of some secret societies. He was pleased that his own subjects did not engage themselves in such activities for, if they did, they wouldn't know what had hit them. And boy, would they remain hit!

'Here, have a look.' He passed the paper to one of his relieved officials. He read the passage that his Chief pointed out and, horrified by what it contained, passed the paper on to his colleagues.

As they busied themselves with the paper, muttering to each other briefly, or swearing softly, the Chief explored his huge agbada pocket for a pack of Benson and Hedges. As he lit the cigarette, he crossed one leg over the other and looked up at the road some metres away to see if there was any sign of an important visitor in a flashy car. There was no such car in sight at all.

The paper was at last returned to him, accompanied by sympathetic cries.

'Really, the Government should do something—something more drastic about these secret societies,' the Chief began. 'Do you know what they are? Ah, they are deadly organisations, murderous, I dare say. Some of them are political associations, some other nasty business.'

He paused, and looked up at the road again for any sign of a car. He had his reasons for doing so. Earlier on, he had boasted to his officials that at least three men would visit him in long, fine cars this very day.

'Your Highness,' said one of the officials. 'To my way of thinking, people join secret societies because of their search for wealth and prestige. Naira today make the average Nigerian go crazy. Our people love money. Yet many are not willing to work for it. Only lazy people join secret societies. People with no confidence in themselves. But what I find most baffling, your Highness, is the way some secret societies employ strange, supernatural powers. Just some months ago, one of these secret societies threatened the manager of a private firm in Plateau State. The organisers said they saw in the stars, or some such place, that the manager was cheating his employees. They threatened to kill the manager if he failed to improve the working conditions of his workers. And, good God!' the man laughed at the memory, 'the manager responded positively to the threat. Instead of calling the police, he gave his employees motor-cycle loans and a salary increment of ₦10 each the next month!'

There was a roar of laughter from the others. But the chief neither laughed or smiled. In fact, he did not even notice what was going on. His sharp hearing had picked up something that sounded like a motor car. He listened carefully. To concentrate better, he threw away the rest of the cigarette that he held in his hand. He listened. The sound was there all right.

Seconds later, the car turned up and headed straight for the palace. The evening sun reflected on the body and windscreen, giving it a smooth, shiny look. But when it neared, the Chief could identify traces of dust on the light-blue air-conditioned 504 GL. Two officials, at the command of the Chief, had already run forward to welcome the important guest.

The driver of the car rolled down the window and switched off the air-conditioner. Two officials opened the car door, helped the guest out and led him towards the Chief. As he walked, the visitor looked round at the surroundings, at the rows of thatched houses, neatly arranged and widely spaced apart.

The Chief could not say who the tall, well-built young man was. But he felt there was something faintly familiar about him, about the way he walked with his head thrust slightly forward in an almost aggressive manner.

The young man greeted the Chief and sat in the arm chair beside him.

'No offence meant, son,' the Chief beamed, 'but I wonder where I know you from? Could you...?'

The visitor rubbed his hands together. 'I'm Mansir, your Highness. Can you have forgotten me so easily? Don't you remember me coming here two years ago?'

Recognition dawned on the Chief and his face split into a grin. 'You mean you are actually Mansir, the son of Bodo, my late subject? God! You have changed greatly, son. Could any of you here have recog-

nised him?' he asked. His officials shook their heads.
'And you have come all the way from Lagos?' the
Chief asked.

'Yes, your Highness,' Mansir answered. 'I
thought I ought to visit you.'

'Just to visit us! All the way from Lagos State to
Kano State. You are a true son of the land, Mansir.
There are some people who do not forget their people
wherever they go. I would have thought...' He
shrugged. 'How many days are you going to spend
with us?'

'I must leave the day after tomorrow.'

'So soon?'

'I can't help it. I must get back to my work.'

'And where do you work?'

'At a small company. I'm a clerk there.'

'But you are obviously really enjoying yourself! A
car... do you have a house?'

'Yes, a two bedroom flat. My wife has recently
delivered.'

'A boy or a girl?'

'A boy. We call him Shamsiddeen.'

'Well, you must be very tired after such a long
journey,' the Chief remarked. He turned to his officials. 'Please will one of you take Mansir to my
special quarters. And don't forget his luggage in the
car.' He turned back to Mansir. 'I'll meet you there
after you have had enough rest, son.'

After Mansir had gone, the Chief remained silent
for a while, lost in deep thought. Then he said slowly, 'I wonder how Mansir comes to be so rich all of a
sudden. Look at what his father was and remember
how Mansir himself was before he left the village for
Lagos...'

An official cut in. 'Your Highness, you can't compare Kofir with Lagos. There are a lot more opportunities in Lagos.'

'I know,' the Chief said, 'but I've been to big cities myself. You... you used to live in Kano City. Why didn't you get rich?' He shook his head thoughtfully. 'I'm afraid there must be something fishy about that young man. Ah, just remember how he was. He left home with no capital—in fact, without even enough money to feed himself, just about two years ago... and now all this... Do you know how much an air-conditioned Peugeot costs? Do you know how much a flat costs in the congested city of Lagos? Do you know how much the lace material he's wearing costs? The total comes to enough to start a big business!'

'It must do, your Highness. I think Mansir's change of fortune came when that Ibo man—you remember him—the one with the Cortina—er, Mr Ibiang... took him to Lagos. Now see what...'

Then another one of the officials joked, 'It seems, your Highness, we might end up saying that Mansir belongs to one secret society or the other!' There was laughter from everyone.

But something rang a bell in the Chief's head. What the man said could explain Mansir's sudden wealth. He should have thought of it himself. Why, it was probably only a matter of putting two and two together. He lit another cigarette and closed his eyes.

Chapter 2

The whole village talked about Mansir. The Chief's palace became the centre of gossip. Prosperous elders of the village gathered there. Everyone was surprised at the success of the young man.

Another thing baffled the elders. Mansir had made his intention known of taking a young man of the village—Daudu—along with him. Everyone knew of Mansir's hatred for Daudu's father in the past. He was the man who had so cruelly ill-treated Mansir's father and family.

The day arrived when Mansir was to leave and, early in the morning, he went taking Daudu along with him. He had easily persuaded the young village boy into going to Lagos with him—a place where opportunities existed just for the taking—or so Mansir had told him.

Now as he drove along the Kano-Funtua road, Mansir kept glancing regretfully at the once-familiar landscape, at the young boys chasing goats into the bush and at the slimly-built young man sitting beside him. He felt jumpy and hot, and was glad of the cool comfort of the air-conditioner. Every now and then he would shudder. His eyes gradually turned red and there was a film of sweat on his forehead as he visualised himself, a dagger in his hand, killing Daudu. Murder. Murderer. The Black

Temple. It did not seem real. Daudu didn't seem to notice anything amiss. Already the rocking car and comforting coolness were lolling him to sleep.

Mansir sat upright as he tried to think of himself as a murderer. Well, actually, he wasn't. He was only taking revenge, a duty he owed to his father and family... Slowly the painful memories of his childhood began to form pictures in his mind, full of all the people that had ill-treated his parents, memories that could make him do anything...

It had been a hot, sunny day. The village lay silent as it always did at noon. Mansir, then a young boy, had been giving a helping hand to his father who worked on the garden of the Alhaji who was Daudu's father. He always felt resentful when he saw the way his father treated the fruits with as much tenderness as if the garden were his own. Mansir, who knew that his father got nothing in return for his honest service but insufficient food and accommodation in a wretched house, was silently grumbling when three of the eleven sons of Alhaji rushed into the garden. The boys were notorious and Mansir silently hoped that they wouldn't do anything to his father.

'Gardener,' cried one, as the others watched. 'Pick some guavas for us!'

'Your father wouldn't like it,' Mansir's father said mildly, pausing from his work. 'Didn't he beat you the other day for picking tomatoes?'

He was right, and Alhaji had warned him not to allow any of his sons into the garden again.

'But it's our father's garden. It's ours as well!' one protested, searching the ground for a piece of stone. The boy was Daudu.

'Okay, if you go and ask—' the old man didn't finish the sentence. Something sharp hit him directly in his right eye, and stars seemed to explode around him. He started to sway. Crying, Mansir rose and helped his father home.

That night his father told him all his grievances. There was a limit to what any man could endure and it was certain that, for him, this limit had been crossed over.

As he talked, the old man's hand kept going to and from the injured eye which by then was very swollen. A colourless liquid kept streaming down his cheek.

'You are young and able, Mansir. Don't let your life be a waste like mine. Since your mother died, I've not been able to look after you and your sister properly. Even though you are the younger one, you must go into the world. But make sure you do so only after your sister's marriage. Go to the city, anywhere where you can earn a reasonable living and live comfortably and independently.' The old man stressed the last word. 'If someone stamps on you don't hesitate to stamp on him in return. Don't allow yourself to be cheated and abused like me...'

About a month later, Mansir's father became seriously ill and died. He died a one-eyed man. A few weeks later Alhaji forced Mansir and his sister out of their wretched home. Mansir's sister had no alternative but to become a prostitute. Mansir got what food and shelter he could.

One evening, the Chief had a very important but unknown guest. The visitor aroused special interest because of his car, a Ford Cortina. He was short and fat, with a thick upper lip, and said his name was

Ibiang. He said he was an Ibo man and that he had been advised by his doctor to get some fresh air in the country. He worked with a big manufacturing company, he told them, situated at Lagos. He didn't know, he said, almost pleadingly, if the Chief could help him with accommodation for a few days—five at the most?

The whole village talked of the important guest. Mansir himself met Ibiang at the palace, little knowing he was the man who would so dramatically change his life.

Normally, as with most young men, Mansir often went to the palace to greet the Chief. But no one could say what actually caused Ibiang and Mansir to become intimate in the short space of only a few days. Perhaps it was because, when Mansir had greeted the Chief, he would find a place away from the people and sit down alone, which attracted Ibiang's attention. Or perhaps it was because of the way he walked with his head thrust forward in an almost aggressive manner, giving him an air of determination.

On his fourth day in the village, Ibiang called Mansir to the 'special quarters' of the Chief.

'Would you like to work in the city, Mansir?' Ibiang asked abruptly.

Mansir was dumbfounded. He hadn't expected such a question from Ibiang. 'I would surely like to, Mr Ibiang,' he answered at last.

'Any city?'

Mansir thought of his father's advice about his sister. But the girl was already a prostitute in Kano City. What could he do about her?

'Yes, Mr Ibiang. Anywhere.'

'Even Lagos?'

'Yes. As long as there are opportunities.'

'There are indeed good opportunities. I want to help you, Mansir. I hope you are glad.'

'Yes I am, thank you.'

Ibiang looked hard at Mansir. 'Are you religious?' he asked.

'Yes, but not very.'

'Would you like to become a member of... er... an organisation which is like a religion... I mean, with its own creed but not really religious?'

'It would be better than staying here,' Mansir said simply.

'Good.' Ibiang looked pleased. 'Now I'll be frank with you. It's a secret society.'

Mansir thought for a while. He didn't really know what secret societies were except that some people were against them. But what had he to lose?

'Where does it operate?' he asked.

'Lagos.'

'Doesn't it have a name?'

'It certainly has,' Ibiang answered. 'It is called "The Black Temple".'

They went to Lagos the next day.

Lagos made Mansir's eyes open wide. Lagos, the city of contrasts, with its slow-moving traffic; hotels of international standard; underground gambling joints; well-organised criminals; tough, efficient policemen; the sea and sea breeze; the innumerable brothels and night clubs; the good and the bad.

Mansir's eyes opened wider when he reached Ibiang's house which was number 15, Amont Estate, Lagos. The estate had all the blessings of luxury. It contained some twenty fine, four-

15

bedroomed bungalows, widely spaced apart. A fine network of narrow well-tarred roads ran through the entire estate. There were three gigantic swimming pools, which were floodlit at night; many beautiful lawns and well-kept gardens. There was even a standby electric-generator in case of a blackout.

Ibiang's wife was dead (she had been killed during the civil war) and he lived with his niece, Marian. Mansir and Ibiang bathed, and then went into the sitting-room, which looked as majestic as a palace. A Persian rug covered the room from wall to wall. In one corner stood a 24″ colour TV set and on top of it was a video tape-recorder. All the rooms were air-conditioned.

'I think we had better start to talk business,' Mansir said eagerly. The house had impressed him and he was only too eager to start earning his own money. Perhaps one day he, too, might be living in such a house, he thought excitedly.

'Yes, the sooner the better,' Ibiang said. 'We will go to the Temple tomorrow at midnight. Don't be afraid of what the Father—we call the head the Father—don't be afraid of what he shows you or tells you.' He glanced at his watch. It showed 11.30 p.m. Marian had already gone to bed.

'You'd better go to bed now,' Ibiang suggested, showing Mansir to a comfortable, well-furnished bedroom. 'Here's your room.'

After Mansir had gone to bed, Ibiang reached for the telephone. 'Is that you Father?'

'Yes. Who is it?' asked an authoritative-sounding voice.

'It's me, Ibiang. I've just returned.'

'I know, I heard. Have you found the right man?'

16

'Yes, Father, I'm sure I have. From the look of it he'll be very loyal and hardworking.'

The illuminated signboard, fixed high up on the wall, read: THE AMOTO PEOPLE'S CHURCH. The Ford Cortina U-turned and pulled up. Two doors were flung open and two gentlemen leapt out and hurriedly headed for the door of the church.

The night was cool and moonless, but several stars shone brightly. The gentle breeze that normally came with the early hours of the morning was refreshing. The sound of sea waves lapping against the sand could be heard faintly.

Ibiang, his peaked cap firmly placed on his head, knocked at the door and waited. Behind him stood Mansir. He felt curious, expectant and almost excited. He was going to be initiated into the Black Temple this very morning.

'Why, Ibiang, it's a church,' Mansir whispered.

'In our business we have to be very careful. Anyway, you'll soon know everything. You have to be sworn into the organisation first.'

The door opened with a 'click' and a strong-looking man allowed them into the church.

Mansir watched Ibiang walk ahead past the rows of benches. He stopped at a door, knocked and removed his shoes.

'The beginning of the rituals,' Mansir thought gloomily, and did the same. He hated rituals, but now that he was joining a secret society, he must force himself to like them.

The door swung back silently and Ibiang beckoned Mansir to follow him.

They walked along a short, narrow corridor. At the end of it, they stopped and knocked at a door. The murmur of the sea could be heard distinctly.

A tall thin man, dressed entirely in black, allowed them into a big dimly lit hall.

'You're to wait here,' the tall man told Ibiang. He led Mansir further into the hall towards a door ahead. Obviously, this man was the 'Father'.

They entered a small dark room and he motioned to Mansir to sit down.

'You are sure that you want to join us?' the Father asked, looking hard at Mansir.

'Yes,' Mansir answered. His heart was banging against his chest at an alarming pace.

'Then let me remind you that ours is a secret society. I'll tell you a few things about it then we'll go back to the hall where you'll be sworn in.'

The Father paused, regarded Mansir for a while, and continued, 'Ours is a big organisation, with branches in many parts of the country. Economically, we are the strongest society in the whole of Lagos. Politically, we are the most influential. One of the main businesses is smuggling. For instance, we smuggle gold from Ghana, diamonds from Sierra Leone and cement from the Republic of Benin. We have been in this business for a long time but none of our members has ever been caught. This is partly because we have influence and partly because of the supernatural powers we employ. We also employ evil. We have found that to satisfy the self, one must employ evil. By joining us you have bade goodbye to most of your worries and problems. But let me warn you here and now that we don't guarantee anything. For safety reasons members do not expose themselves to one another except when necessary.'

The Father paused again, dipped his hand into a deep pocket and took out a sharp knife. He handed it to Mansir. 'Let's go back to the hall now,' he said.

His heart thumping loudly, Mansir followed the tall man back to the hall. At the first corner they stopped. Before them stood a row of drums.

'To show your loyalty, you'll have to let some of your blood.' The Father spoke softly. 'Don't be afraid, I'll instruct you.' He took Mansir's right hand in his and turned it until the knife he had given him was pointing at his left hand.

'Now! Cut your flesh! Cut it! Cut it!' His voice was soft but insistent.

Mansir obeyed as if in a trance. He felt a sharp pain as the blade cut into his palm. Then he repeated the words of the oath after the Father.

'I swear to be a faithful member of the Black Temple. I am ready to sacrifice myself for its cause. If, at any time in my life, I betray the Black Temple or in any way act against it, may my throat be cut and my blood be let out as it was from my palm.'

Mansir could hear the drip, drip of the blood as drops fell on one of the drums. His eyes showed his pain and fear, and the way he perspired showed how nervous and ill at ease with the whole situation he was. Only one thought made him control himself: the thought of living in a house as luxurious as Ibiang's.

On the Father's order, he started to beat the drum that had his blood smeared on it. Each beat produced an eerie sensation that crept up his spine. As he continued to beat the drum mechanically, the sound gradually became a distant echo and it was as if he was unaware of what he was doing.

'Stop!' The Father's voice cut into his consciousness and he shivered. He didn't know if he would have lost consciousness had he not been stopped just in time. He wiped his sweaty face with his bloodstained hand and straightened up.

The Father's voice was sharp now. 'And don't ever think of betraying us. We often detect a person before he betrays us. We have the power to kill a member living miles away from us without it being necessary for us to be physically present. This is because we employ voodooism. To some extent we can also predict the future, thanks to our knowledge of astrology. What's your star?'

'Cancer.' Ibiang had warned Mansir that he would be asked this question.

'Right. You are now a member. The only things we require from you are hard, honest work and regular sacrifices. Your friend will tell you the details of our rules and regulations and, of course, of your job. This is your starting salary.' He showed Mansir a piece of paper.

The figures Mansir saw on the paper made him breathless. Why, with that amount of money he could paint the whole of Lagos red!

'Where do I find Ibiang?' he asked huskily.

'At the end of the corridor.'

He found Ibiang, who congratulated him on his initiation and assured him that he would get many profitable returns. Then Ibiang led him towards a door that opened on to the back of the building and faced the sea directly.

'Where do we go now?' Mansir asked, tending his

wounded hand.

'I'm going to show you a part of your work. Do you know how to handle a motor boat?'

'No.'

'Then come with me.'

They walked towards the seashore where Mansir could make out the shapes of boats that were fastened to a long wooden jetty.

This marked Mansir's entry into the business of smuggling and the many other hideous activities of the Black Temple. Mansir, of course, had no reason to suspect that it was the hope of the Black Temple to have him so well trained that he would, one day, be able to become its representative in Kano State.

The Black Temple had its eyes on the uranium deposits in the Republic of Niger and it was already making preparations to start business with other smugglers on the other side of the border.

Mansir, it was hoped, would be the link in their transactions.

Now, as he thought of the things that had happened, Mansir wiped the sweat that had gathered on his forehead and told himself to concentrate on the road. He was eager to reach Lagos and make the human sacrifice the Black Temple had required from him.

Chapter 3

Mansir's flat was located at No. 25A Creedy Avenue, Lagos. It was a nicely-built two-bedroom flat overlooking a river with a dead end.

As soon as he had come home that evening, Mansir knew that there was something wrong with his wife. He knew from the way she kept glancing at him questioningly as they sat in the sitting room talking to Daudu, who had arived at Mansir's invitation, that she was nervous and that something was frightening her. In the latter part of the evening, during dinner, she talked more freely to Daudu, which was very unusual as Daudu was a stranger to her. This was an unwelcome development for Mansir did not want his wife to be fully acquainted with Daudu. He had invited Daudu to Lagos for a particular purpose and only he knew what fate lay in store for him.

They watched TV for some time. All the time Mansir could feel his wife's tenseness like dew in the early morning air. Around 9.00 p.m. he went into their bedroom and a moment later Susanna, his wife, followed with their son, Shamsiddeen, cradled in her arms.

'Are you going to bed?' his wife asked him, putting the baby down on the bed and starting to rock it to sleep.

'No, I don't think so,' Mansir answered, eyeing Susanna. Her tall, slim figure, her large, widely-spaced eyes, her straight nose and small, white even teeth always fascinated him. 'Just going to change and have a shower,' he continued, moving towards the clothes closet.

'Do you know anything about the telephone calls?' Susanna asked softly.

Mansir was about to unzip his trousers, but he stopped, suddenly rigid with attention.

'Telephone calls?' he asked, alarmed.

'I mean, were you expecting any telephone calls while you were away? The caller never gave a name. I don't like anonymous calls. Who could it have been?' she enquired further. She could see that her husband was worried. When Mansir didn't answer, she continued, 'Oh, Mansir, I'm your wife, but sometimes you frighten me with your ways. One part of you is still mysterious to me. You often spend days away from home; often get called in the middle of the night ... odd things at odder hours ... Mansir, why don't you share your secrets with me? Remember I'm your wife, the only person who is really intimate with you. Would you rather confide in other people, like the gardener who waters all the gardens outside but his own?' She looked up intently at Mansir with bright, innocent eyes, eyes that wanted to explore more than they were supposed to know.

Mansir came over and sat down beside her, taking her hands into his. 'I ... I just don't know what to say,' he stammered.

This was not the first time his wife had complained. He had always tried to hide his membership of the Black Temple from her. He did not want her to know that he was a first class smuggler and very much part of the machinery of organised crime in Lagos. More than that, disclosing any information about the Black Temple to anyone other than members amounted to betrayal. He still remembered the oath he had taken during his initiation—'I swear to be a faithful member of the Black Temple. I am ready to sacrifice myself for its cause. If, at anytime in my life, I betray the Black Temple, or in any way act against it, may my throat be cut and my blood be let out as it was from my palm.'

The oath, however, was not the only reason why he wouldn't betray the Temple. He was determined to take revenge on a society that had so mutilated him and his family. The Black Temple was the best instrument for achieving this notable aim.

'My dear, you've got the whole thing confused,' he said at last. 'And you're tired. You should be in bed by now. What with the housework and the child to look after ... But tell me about these telephone calls. What was said?'

Susanna withdrew her hands from his. 'Well, the phone would just ring, I would pick it up and an authoritative-sounding voice would ask "Is this Mansir's residence?" I would answer, "Yes," and enquire who the caller was. But the voice would only ask, "Has Mansir returned?" When I answered, "No," the man, or whoever it was, would hang up. There were seven such calls, Mansir—two in the middle of the night.'

There was now no doubt about it. The caller was the Father, the pastor of the Amoto People's Church, chief organiser of the Black Temple.

Mansir stood up and began to pace restlessly about the room. At last he stopped and took Susanna gently in his arms. He could feel her body trembling. He would have to find some means of quieting her nerves and washing away her accumulated fears. But he knew from experience not to try and appeal to her body, only to her reason.

'You've no cause to be nervous or afraid of anything,' Mansir murmured in a voice he could hardly identify as his own. 'Trust me as a loving wife should trust her husband. And forgive me if I seem to be aloof at any time.'

'Oh! I'm sorry, I nearly forgot another call, entirely different from the others,' Susanna said, pushing Mansir gently away. 'Ibiang telephoned. He said you should hurry and meet him as soon as you got back. Actually, he telephoned twice and ... and he seemed to be anxious.'

'Good God!' cried Mansir weakly. The affair was getting more and more serious, if not sinister. 'Go to sleep now, Susanna,' he said, patting her, 'I'll go straight round to him.'

'What, at this time of the night?' She glanced at the wall clock, which read 10.45. 'Can't you leave it till tomorrow?'

'You never know, Susanna. It should be a golden rule always to finish what you can finish today. Now, for God's sake, don't go on worrying yourself. Be loyal and go to sleep.' He kissed her gently.

He went out hurriedly to his car and was turning the ignition key in the lock when he saw the light in their bedroom go off. Daudu, however, was still in the sitting room glued to the TV set.

As he drove along in the thinning traffic, he tried

to deceive himself that nothing was amiss. But he could not prevent a creepy sensation running up his spine every now and then.

Mansir found Ibiang in his big sitting room, sipping occasionally from a glass of beer which was on the table in front of him. Ibiang was fully dressed and the blue peaked cap was on his head as usual. The big house was silent and most of it was in darkness. The only light came from the single lamp in the sitting room.

'Why, it's very dark in here,' Mansir said. 'Do you want me to switch on more lights?'

'No,' Ibiang answered in a surprisingly calm voice, in spite of the alcohol. 'There's no one about in the house. Marian is in bed already.'

'What is it you wanted to see me for?' Mansir asked, sinking into a deep sofa.

'It's the Temple, Mansir. I don't know why they are so anxious about you.' Ibiang took another sip of his beer and looked intently at Mansir for a while. 'Have you found the man?'

Mansir shuddered. 'Yes.'

'Otherwise, I could have helped you. The Temple runs a fleet of taxis. That way it is always easy to find a victim for any ritual or sacrifice. Pretty smart, don't you think?'

Mansir nodded to show his approval, then suddenly frowned. 'But what's so important about these sacrifices?'

'I didn't expect such a question from you,' Ibiang answered curtly. 'But I suppose it is not surprising that you should ask. The Black Temple, my dear friend, is as mysterious to me as it is to you. Don't tell me that I've spent more years with the Temple than you. Hell, it seems to me that the more years you spend with the organisiation, the more mysterious it becomes. Though I am older and more senior in the Temple than you, all I know about it are its smuggling rackets, night clubs, the invisible lawyers, flocks of politicians and rich men who are, as you already know, members. I also know about the gambling joints and the like. One thing is clear, however,' he said, refilling his glass. 'There are only a very few men at the top who engineer the lines of action and get all the profit. These people are as invisible as air and there is no way you can get at them. Only the Father knows them. There are those of us who do the actual work and are paid enough money to buy a nice car and pay for an equally nice house.' Ibiang looked around him, his face splitting into a grin. His gaze rested briefly on the Persian rug that covered the floor from wall to wall. 'As I said, the Temple is mysterious. Some say it has strange, supernatural powers. Others deny it. Personally, I believe that what the Temple is trying to do is to condition the lives of its members the way it wants—so that they become operating machines, mechanical human beings. The sacrifices are, and this is also a personal view, tests of loyalty. Committing a deadly crime like murder is the most severe test for any man—except, of course, committing suicide. Those who have tried to avoid the sacrifices in the past, or to outsmart the Temple, have always met with the ultimate penalty—death.'

Murder! Mansir could feel the sweat running down him like the tributaries of a river.

'And they rang you to caution me?' he asked.

'Sure. To speed things up.'

'Help me, Ibiang,' Mansir appealed. 'I'm in great need of help.' He told Ibiang abut his wife and baby and his anxiety about them getting involved. When he had finished, he said, 'Please give me a drink.'

'No.' Ibiang spoke harshly, his eyes hardening suddenly. 'You don't drink and you're not starting now. Beer is of no use to anyone — and that includes me. It'll only ruin you.'

'I'm not taking beer,' Mansir said, reaching for a glass nearby. Ibiang tried to stop him but, on seconds thoughts, changed his mind.

'Whisky,' Mansir spoke firmly. 'And I'm a man,' he asserted, draining his glass and reaching for more.

Sometime later, Mansir rose to go. He was swaying a little. 'Oh, it is much, much too late,' he cried. 'My wife will know that I'm up to something. She'll smell the whisky on me. Oh, Ibiang—'

'Hey, just a moment,' Ibiang said, getting to his feet. 'They want you at the Temple now,' he said, his voice full of menace.

Mansir reacted as if someone had slapped him. He managed to control himself after a few minutes, mumbled a curt good night and left.

After Mansir had gone, Ibiang calmly reached for the telephone, dialled some numbers and began to speak hurriedly. Afterwards he settled down and patiently waited for three o'clock to come. At that time he was due to leave for the waterfront to take delivery of some goods he was expecting from a neighbouring country.

Chapter 4

It was one of those rainy mornings in Lagos when it rained lightly for fifteen minutes or so, then stopped and, after a while, started all over again. During the brief intervals of sunshine a cool breeze blew over the island from the Atlantic.

A body had been discovered that morning.

The first to spot it was Police Constable Warreau Micky, who was attached to the Linivia Island Police. Constable Micky was returning to his small bed-sitter after finishing his night duty at Queen Amina Avenue, where he guarded a high-ranking police officer. As he hurried along the pavement, his rifle firmly clutched under his arm, he was thinking to himself how irrational some policies were. He couldn't see the rationale of one man guarding another. It meant that some people were more important and more equal than others—so that he had to spend the night under the bare—now rainy—sky, to protect someone else who slept inside without knowing where his head was!

Micky, a man of average build, with alert-looking eyes, was ambitious without being competent. His small bed-sitter worried him. He would have preferred to live in a one-bedroom apartment with a kitchenette. But he could not afford this on his meagre salary. He desperately wanted promotion and was always on the lookout for opportunities, but somehow he usually failed to see them when they appeared.

The Johnson-Highbridge junction where he stopped daily for a taxi was near at hand. Looking up, he could see a vulture or two circling lazily round a fixed spot. Micky's eyes instinctively searched the ground and what he saw, even at that distance, made something inside his stomach turn over and brought the bile into his mouth.

Forgetting about all his worries, Micky half walked and half ran to the spot. Spreadeagled on the pavement was the body of a young man, his face facing the sky and his hands spread out as if in supplication. Except for a pair of tight underpants, the body was naked. There was a deep cut in the chest, and another smaller one on the side of the neck. Even the sudden flurry of rain could not wash away the blood that had spread about the body.

Micky, a handkerchief held against his mouth, surveyed the body and cursed under his breath. He was careful not to touch anything until he could bring the whole dreadful matter to the notice of his superiors.

He saw a prison van coming along the road and waved frantically at it to stop. He barked instructions to the curious and baffled driver. 'Don't just sit there staring! Hurry off to the police station and tell them what I told you!'

The driver engaged the gears and looked once more at the mutilated body by the roadside before he drove off. Micky lit a cigarette and waited for the police, waving motorists on and keeping passers-by away from the body. This could possibly be the opportunity he was looking for, he comforted himself.

Shortly afterwards, a police Land Rover pulled up by the body. The front door was flung open and a tall, lean and handsome man, Inspector Nur of the Linivia Island Police, leapt out. He was followed by several policemen.

Inspector Nur was rumoured to be one of the most brilliant and tough policemen in the whole of Lagos. The unit he was attached to—the Linivia Island Police—was famous for its success in bringing the master criminals to book.

The police crowded around the body while, after talking briefly to Constable Micky, Inspector Nur knelt down to examine it more closely. His searching eyes told him that the wound in the chest led to the heart and that the carotid artery in the neck had been cut. He did not miss the three artificially made cowrie shells that were fastened to the left hand of the dead man. Written on each of the cowrie shells were the two letters B and T.

What could BT mean, Inspector Nur wondered, as he looked over the body again for any signs of identification. The dead young man had neither noticeable scars nor any tribal marks anywhere on him.

'Sergeant Andrews,' he called, getting up. 'Go over to the Land Rover and call for the police ambulance.'

'Yes, sir.' The short, fat man left.

Pressmen had arrived on the scene and were taking pictures of the dead body. Some tried to interview Nur, but he respectfully ignored them. He had, however, been careful enough to unfasten the cowrie shells before any pictures of them were taken.

An ambulance pulled up a moment later, and the body came under the control of the police doctor. Some minutes passed while the examination took place and then the body was placed on a stretcher and carried into the ambulance.

After a last-minute inspection of the place, Nur and his men drove off to the Linivia Island Police Headquarters. There, Inspector Nur went straight up to Chief Biodun's office, to inform the Chief of the details of the body—surely this was a case of murder?

Chief Biodun was the head of the police unit and Nur dreaded to think what his reaction might be when he heard the news. The Chief was known to get very emotional about murder cases. Suspects always had a rough time with him during interrogation.

'Damn it, this is advertised murder,' the Chief cried, banging his fist on the well-polished desk. He stood up, his massive frame and the grey hair around the temples exuding an air of authority. 'And no clues, not a single clue?' he continued, eyeing Inspector Nur as if he was the murderer.

'No, not many clues, sir,' Nur began, rubbing his hands together, 'but there were three artificial cowrie shells fastened to the dead man's left hand.'

'Cowrie shells?' the Chief repeated, looking down at him.

Nur placed a handkerchief on the desk. 'They are in there, sir. BT is scribbled on each one.'

Chief Biodun, who was still standing and about to untie the handkerchief, seemed immediately to go limp. He flopped back on his chair. Almost lazily, he took a handkerchief out of his breast pocket and wiped away the sweat that had started to form on his forehead. Carefully, he untied the handkerchief that lay before him on the desk and began to examine the three artificially-made cowrie shells.

Nur watched with a mixed feeling of fear and interest. He had never seen the Chief behave this way before.

'Well, we can't take this as a clue,' the Chief said at last, breathing heavily. 'Please ring for coffee.'

Coffee arrived, and a police constable poured them two cups.

'We might need these one day,' Nur said, taking a sip. 'The initials could mean something, though. I wonder if ...' The Chief growled.

Nur stood up, realising that the Chief did not wish to continue the conversation. 'I'm going over to my office to wait for the doctor's report.'

The Chief growled again.

Leaving the cowrie shells on the desk, Nur went down to his office. Chief Biodun's reaction was rather unusual today. Nur couldn't help noticing the change. The old man seemed almost nervous. Really, the news of the mutilated body had shaken his composure a good deal, Nur thought.

The *Daily Mirror,* the evening newspaper the Linivia Island police trusted most, carried a picture of the mutilated body. The police invited anyone who knew the dead young man to come forward and identify him.

That evening, Mansir drove to the Linivia Island Police Headquarters. He was shown to the morgue where he identified the dead man. It was none other than Daudu.

As he drove away after having identified Daudu's body, Mansir couldn't help thinking back to how he had stabbed Daudu. He remembered Daudu's surprised look and then the look of terror and pain that followed as he gradually came to terms with death. At the last minute, Mansir had cursed himself several times for what he had done—and yet had done to a society that had once humiliated him. He also reminded himself that it had been Daudu who had made his father a one-eyed man. But without any conscious effort, the thought drove itself out of his mind.

Would he like his son—Shamsiddeen—to be like him? he asked himself. No, he wouldn't. To be like him was to be a murderer, and a partner in organised crime.

Every now and then he would ponder at the possibility of the police catching up with him. Then he would reassure himself that he had left no telltale marks at the scene. There was no way in which the murder could be linked to him.

After driving about aimlessly for a while, Mansir pulled up by a small night club where he ordered a whisky. He had many problems to sort out in his mind. What explanation, for instance, would he give his now suspicious wife about Daudu's sudden and brutal death? Lots of whisky. That was the answer.

Meanwhile, Inspector Nur was sitting in his office, going carefully through the report he had prepared on the murder case. On his right side was a cup of coffee—his second cup since breakfast that morning —from which he sipped occasionally. The two inspectors he shared the room with were out and he had the room to himself.

He was about to file away the report when someone knocked at the door.

'Come in,' he said softly, as he took the last sip of coffee. The door opened and a tall, thin, impressive-looking man wearing a doctor's uniform came into the room.

'Hello, doctor,' Nur said. 'Have a seat, please. I've been waiting for your report.'

The police doctor drew up a chair and sat down. 'Had a hectic day, huh?' he said chattily, taking a piece of paper out of his jacket pocket. He placed it carefully on the table in front of Nur. 'Sorry to have kept you waiting. I finished this report about an hour ago but the wife telephoned, you know, and I had to go home.'

What of his own wife? Nur thought almost in a panic, reaching for the report. He had totally forgotten about her. To think they had been married only four months ago! Anyway, he would telephone her after going through the doctor's report.

'Well, I must leave now,' the doctor said, getting to his feet. 'If you want anything further, I'm down at the lab.'

'Thanks a lot, doc.' Nur's attention was already concentrated on the report, which was brief and to the point. The cause of death had been loss of blood. The carotid artery had been cut. There was a deep cut in the chest. The heart was missing. The weapon used could have been a 15 centimetre-long serrated kitchen knife. The time of death was between four to five in the morning.

Cowrie shells, heart missing, loss of blood ...

could the young man have been the victim of some religious sect or ritual? Nur chewed the facts over in his mind. And BT ... what could those initials mean?

Inspector Nur stared regretfully at the empty cup by his side. A moment later a knock sounded on the door and Sergeant Andrews came into the office and sat down.

'Hello,' Sergeant Andrews said conversationally. 'Is that the doc's report that you're reading?'

'Yes, Andy. From the look of things this case will present problems—cowrie shells, missing heart ... and still we are not able to get any suspects. Just a mutilated body by the roadside—that's all we've got. It's like a hit and run case. To my way of thinking, there's either a religious sect or a secret society involved in this case. I think my preference is to believe that we are dealing with a secret society.'

'Yes, you could be right, Inspector. I wonder what the meaning of the initials on the cowrie shells could be?'

'That's what baffles me most. If it is a secret society, would they advertise the murder? Would they not prefer to remain anonymous?'

Andrews shook his head. 'Are you going to file the reports away and mark the case "Open" until some better evidence turns up?'

'I don't know,' Nur answered. 'I just can't say. If I could have solved the murder mystery today, I would have done it. But there are no clues. And the Chief has not been very encouraging either.'

'That's very unusual for him. Personally, I wouldn't want to tamper with a religious sect or a secret society. They often possess spiritual powers.

Their members could possibly be the top, influential people you see driving around in flashy cars. A wink from them is enough to keep you out of police work—for ever and for good.'

'So the thing to do is to sit down and watch them killing innocent souls?' Nur snapped.

'Sorry, sir.' Andrews stood up. 'I'm going home now. Been in this hole since morning.'

As Andrews headed for the door, Nur reached for the telephone and dialled his home number. His wife answered and, as he expected, nearly blew the top of his head off with angry words.

After locking the car in the garage, Mansir mounted the stairs leading to his front door. His wife met him at the door and followed him into the bedroom.

'You are drunk,' she said accusingly, after helping him to lie comfortably on the bed.

'No ... I'm not drunk. I don't drink. It's my stomach ... think I have fever,' he mumbled incoherently.

'Don't lie to me, Mansir. It's no use whatsoever. Just look at how you are perspiring! Anyway, I can smell the alcohol on you!'

She edged closer to him, and sat on the edge of the bed, running her fingers up and down his face.

'I know you are up to something, Mansir. No, don't protest. I don't need any explanation now. Just go to sleep and wake up fresh.'

'Mum!' Shamsiddeen their son cried from the sitting room, 'Mum!' The child began to cry.

'Let me attend to the baby, Mansir. He's just woken up from his sleep.'

Patting her husband lightly she hurried off to the sitting room.

On the bed, Mansir turned on his side and felt a tear roll along his nose.

He couldn't remember when last he cried.

The Black Temple was really trying to ruin him now. The police would be on his trail—if only they could identify it. His home was gradually losing its warmth—and he was as mysterious to his wife as the Black Temple was to him.

Why choose him of all people?

What had he done to be asked to provide a human sacrifice? Could they have doubted his loyalty?

His mind was still whirling when he fell into a restless sleep full of nightmarish dreams.

The next morning, after a nice shower and a hearty breakfast, Mansir and his wife sat in the sitting room, talking only when necessary. Mansir cradled Shamsiddeen in his arms. The child was playing with a doll.

After a while, Susanna left her seat and sat beside Mansir.

'Mansir,' she began, looking up at him. 'Do you really love me?'

Mansir looked away. 'I do, very much.'

'And you trust me as well?'

'I should. You're my wife.'

'But do you really?' She was insistent.

'Yes, Susanna. I trust you. To God.'

'Then why don't you open your heart to me? Why don't you tell me what's wrong?'

'There is ... nothing wrong, Susanna.'

'Then why have you started drinking recently?'

Mansir looked down at his son. The child looked

up and laughed, showing him the baby doll.

'Susanna,' he said slowly, 'I'm a troubled man. I guess it has to do with my poor background.' He enveloped her hand gently into his. 'Help me, Susanna. This is the only place where I can get some comfort and feel some confidence. Don't deny me these, my dear.'

'What will you tell Daudu's people now?' she enquired after a pause.

'That he's dead, of course. What more can I say?'

'Killed, you mean.'

Mansir cringed. 'I know ... I know ... but ...'

'You left together around three in the morning, Mansir.'

Mansir shivered. 'We didn't leave together ... I couldn't sleep so I got up and went and looked inside his room. But he was not there and I was worried. So I went to search for him and...'

'Forget it, Mansir,' Susanna cut in. 'It's no use. I won't ask you any more questions. I'll just accept you as you are because I love you. Moreover, there's the child to look after. Don't think I'm angry with you. Just forget.'

There was a prolonged silence, then Mansir suddenly asked, his hopes rising, 'How about having a short holiday somewhere away from Lagos?'

Susanna almost brightened. 'Anything out of town would be welcome. That would really be splendid. But where shall we go?'

'I'll surprise you on that,' Mansir smiled, handing the child over to her. 'Let me go and make arrangements. Pack us some clothes. We will leave this very day!' He bent down, kissed her and went out to his car.

As he drove towards the Murtala Mohammed Airport, Mansir cursed himself for not thinking of taking a holiday before. It would have solved some of his problems. He knew that his wife was very keen on going to the Yankari Game Reserve, a holiday resort in Bauchi State, for a holiday. He hoped the holiday would raise her spirits. Two tickets to Kano and then a car to Bauchi State would take them to Yankari in no time, he thought.

He was so occupied with his thoughts that he failed to notice a blue Honda Civic following closely behind him.

At the Airport, he bought two tickets from Lagos to Kano and one return ticket for himself, for he knew only too well that he would have to be back in the evening of the following day for a scheduled meeting with the Black Temple.

The Lagos to Kano plane was due to leave at 23.30 hours.

He drove slowly back to his flat. All the while the blue Honda Civic followed closely behind him, unnoticed.

His wife had already packed the things they would need. She was delighted when he told her where they were to go.

At 10.30, after locking up their flat and putting the car in the garage, they called a taxi to take them to the airport. The taxi was followed by the same blue Honda Civic.

The man driving the Honda Civic was short and thin and he had a scar running down the whole extent of his face, starting from his right eye. At the airport he watched until he saw the plane to Kano take off, then he hurried to one of the many telephone booths in the airport.

'Is that you, Father?' he asked politely.

'Yes,' an authoritative sounding voice answered. 'Do not say your name. I recognise your voice. What's the matter?'

'Mansir and his family have just left in the 23.30 plane to Kano.'

There was a minute's silence.

'I see,' the man at the other end said at last. 'Did you notice if he made any suspicious moves?'

'No, Father. But I'm wondering whether Mansir could have panicked. I mean, do you think he might be frightened of the police after what he has done?'

'Don't worry about that. No policeman can get at him. Our security is intact, our influence and membership wide. Now you can go home. But keep a watch on the airport and his flat. Report personally to me when he returns. You should realise that we must test a person thoroughly before giving him an important post which will bring much heavier responsibility.'

'I do realise that, Father,' he said, but the Father had already hung up.

The small man stepped out of the booth and went to fetch the blue Honda Civic from the parking lot. He was confident of himself and his employers. He knew that wherever Mansir went, he would always be under surveillance. For it was the policy of the Black Temple to test a man thoroughly to be sure of his loyalty and commitment to its cause before giving him a top, senior post.

Chapter 5

Inspector Nur edged his car into the slow-moving traffic. The day was warm and as he drove he wished there was an air-conditioner in the car. Looking at the endless line of cars ahead he thought gloomily that the murderer he was looking for could be in any of the cars or in the streets or, possibly, even out of Lagos.

It was the beginning of the weekend and he was determined to waste no time at the office. He planned to spend the day with his wife on the beach. What with this frustrating case and the unusual attitude of his Chief, he longed to be somewhere out of the reach of his colleagues and the phone.

After thirty minutes of slow driving he finally managed to make it to the office. One of two other inspectors he shared the room with was inside, going through a mass of reports. An empty cup of coffee stood by his side and there was cigarette ash all over his shirt front.

'Good morning, Inspector Hassan,' Nur called, going over to his desk. 'Beginning a hard day?'

'Morning, Nur,' the heartily-built man answered. 'Hey, Nur, what's biting the Chief this morning? Between you and me, he seems to be very thoughtful and rather gloomy. Perhaps something is worrying him. Have you been to his office yet?'

The shrill ring of the telephone interrupted their conversation. Nur picked up the receiver. 'Hello, Nur here,' he said.

'It's me, Sergeant Andrews,' said the man at the other end in an excited voice. 'Something really nasty has happened. Please come over quickly to the Barbeach. I don't think I can handle this alone. I think it could be something to do with what you call the "mysterious murder".'

Nur dropped the receiver and sprang to his feet. 'Please tell the Chief that something has turned up at the Barbeach. I'm going there now.'

Inspector Nur dashed through the door, yelled at a police constable to accompany him, and hurried towards his car.

As he drove furiously towards the beach, despite the traffic, Nur almost cringed at the thought of what Chief Biodun's reaction might be this time. He had begun to feel suspicious about the Chief's attitude. But he was determined to explore this case further. He was determined to uproot the secret society concerned—if indeed it was a secret society.

The Barbeach was crowded with bathers, as it always was at weekends. Colourful sun umbrellas dotted the beach and there were people bathing in the shallow waters at the edge of the sea.

Inspector Nur steered his car with difficulty over the sand towards a police Land Rover some metres away. Standing by the Land Rover was Sergeant Andrews, waving frantically at Nur. There was a crowd forming around the Land Rover and two policemen were trying to push the curious weekenders away. At the centre, by the Land Rover, was something that looked like a human form. It was covered by a white sheet.

Nur pulled up a couple of metres away. He could guess what was under the sheet.

'There.' Andrews pointed. 'But it's terribly messy.' He took out a soiled handkerchief and dabbed at his sweaty face.

Nur nodded, then knelt down and uncovered the body. Horrified, he shrank back from what he saw.

It was the body of a man of about forty. The carotid artery in the neck had been deeply cut in the way that goats were slaughtered. A dark stain covered another deep cut in the chest. Tied to the left hand of the body were three artificial cowrie shells with the initials BT on each of them. Nur untied the cowrie shells and let the piece of cloth drop back over the body.

'No one has tampered with anything, Sir,' Andy said.

'Where did you find it—here?'

'No, deep in the water. A hand was sticking out of the water and a curious bather swam over to see what it really was. He ended up with a body. I was just passing by when some people stopped me and told me what had happened.'

'Okay. Call for the ambulance now.'

While they waited for the ambulance to come, Nur did some thinking. The two 'mysterious murders' corresponded. Both victims had been killed in the same way. He was sure that the autopsy would come up with the same results. There was no doubt now that a secret society was involved. But what clues, what leads had he? Nothing but two dead bodies, six cowrie shells and a cold rebuff from his Chief. Even the local police informers seemed to be quiet. Everyone was quiet...

They had not long to wait before the ambulance appeared, its siren warning the crowd off. The police doctor made a careful examination of the body, then the dead man was placed on a stretcher and the ambulance shot off.

Nur asked Sergeant Andrews to join him in his car and as they drove slowly through the traffic, Andrews began to talk.

'This'll knock the Chief over, I tell you! I've heard he's getting more and more quiet.'

'That's the trouble with him,' Nur said simply, 'but we must break this case. I'm only waiting for some sort of lead.'

'What a mess.'

'What?'

'The body. It was badly mutilated. I'm sorry for what I said about secret societies and being afraid of them. I share your view wholeheartedly now. It is the duty of the police to uproot these harmful and unwanted products of society.'

'But some people do not think that way,' Nur said. He had the Chief in mind. But he could be wrong, he warned himself. He must be careful.

'Yeah, I know that.' Irritated by the slow pace at which they were moving, he added sharply, 'I wish this car had a siren.'

At the Police Headquarters, Nur went up the steep stairs and down the dimly lit corridor that carried a smell that seemed peculiar to police buildings. He knocked once and immediately opened the door to Chief Biodun's office. He knew that a message would already have reached the Chief about the body that had been found on the Barbeach.

'Hello, Chief.' Nur sat down, and placed a handkerchief before Biodun. 'The cowrie shells are in there. If we compare them to those that were found yesterday, I'm sure we'll find they are identical in all respects.'

'Things getting out of control, huh?' the Chief said, a fat cigar burning between his lips. His eyes had the kind of dark rings below them that suggested a lack of sufficient sleep.

'No, not out of control, Chief. Things are under control. We just need a lead.'

The Chief ignored him and brought a handkerchief out of a drawer in his desk. He compared the cowrie shells lying on Nur's handkerchief with those he already had.

They were of the same size, make, and bore the same initials—BT.

'I've been wondering and puzzling over what on earth BT could mean,' said Nur.

The Chief ignored Nur's remark entirely. 'Well, what do you plan to do now?' he barked.

'Perhaps we should send a couple of pictures to the editor of the *Daily Mirror* to see if anyone can help with an identification. We could ask him to put in a short note requesting any person on the beach early this morning—I should say between the hours of three and five a.m.—who happened to notice anything unusual or suspicious, to come here and aid us with information.'

'Don't make a fool of yourself. Why between three and five in the morning? Do you think any sane man would be on the beach at such a time?' the Chief asked mockingly.

'You never know. Strange things often do happen.' Nur excused himself and left Biodun puffing away smoke and occasionally wiping the sweat from his forehead with a dirty handkerchief.

The doctor's report confirmed Nur's guesses. The time of death was the same as the day before, almost the same type of weapon had been used and the bodies bore similar mutilations.

Around 4.30 p.m. a shabby-looking youth walked into the lobby of the Police building. The desk sergeant on duty looked the youth over with contempt, thinking he saw the signs of a junkie or drunkard in him.

'What do you want?' The sergeant spoke sharply.

'I... I want to see Inspector Nur,' the youth replied nervously, twisting his hands and blinking at the strong light.

'What makes you think the Inspector will want to see you?'

'I have some information for him, Sir... I...'

'Information?' the sergeant became alert. 'About what?'

'The murder on the beach.'

The sergeant was convinced. 'See that door, the second on the left? Okay, he's in there. Just knock and go straight in.'

As the youth made for the door, the desk sergeant reached for the internal telephone to notify Inspector Nur.

Inspector Nur told the youth to sit himself comfortably down. From behind his desk he studied the tall, painfully thin boy of about eighteen, who glanced nervously about.

'What do you want to see me for?' Nur asked in a soft, gentle voice.

'You... you advertised in the papers that...'

Nur nodded and smiled encouragingly at the boy, trying to make him feel at ease so that he would talk freely.

'Well, I was on the beach about that time. I fell asleep on the sand.'

Nur realised that the boy was a drug addict, but he said nothing.

The boy continued, 'Around four, I'd say, an unusual roaring sound woke me up. It was a fast-moving motor boat.'

Nur leaned forward, his interest aroused. 'A motor boat?'

'Yes, Inspector. Its light was on. It made a U-turn and then headed back the way it came from.'

'Was anything dropped from the boat? A large parcel, maybe?'

'I don't know, Sir. It was so dark and the motor-boat was quite far away. But I think... I think something could have been dropped. The boat stop-ped for a moment and I thought I heard a splash. That's why I came.'

Nur thanked the boy and escorted him out.

Of course, the body could have been dropped by the boat. Assuming that it was, this fact also pointed to a secret society being involved. Only the rich organisations and a few rich men in Lagos own-ed motor-boats. What could a motor-boat have been doing at about four in the morning?

Inspector Nur went over to the wall where a large map of Lagos was fastened. He traced the location of the beach with a pencil and made dots here and there. When he had finished his examination, he called for Sergeant Andrews. He came into the office promptly.

'Anything up, Sir? The desk sergeant was telling me about—'

'Yes, something has turned up,' Inspector Nur interrupted. 'But it could also be nothing. I want you to take some men with you down to the beach.' He consulted the dots on the map. 'I want a list of all the people and all the organisations who own motor boats between here and here.'

'Is there a possibility that one of these people could be involved?' asked Andrews.

'In our work we have to take chances. At least this has given us an area of investigation which we must follow up.'

Sergeant Andrews saluted and went out.

Nur decided not to tell the Chief about this development until the investigation was over.

About two hours later Sergeant Andrews returned with a list of names running to foolscap length. Inspector Nur's plan was to show the Chief the list without warning. If the list contained the name or location of any secret society of which the Chief had knowledge, Nur believed that by watching his face intently as he read the list, there would be some flicker of recognition or change of expression. Nur had learned of this technique during psychological training at the police college.

He took the list to the Chief and sat down in a strategic position opposite him.

'A professional way of wasting time and resources, I see,' the Chief grumbled as he started to read the list. Chewing a cigar in his mouth, the

Chief had gone half way down the list when he suddenly frowned and his eyebrows rose a fraction. He was gazing intently at a name on the list—The Amoto People's Church. He didn't realise that he had bitten his cigar in two and that the smouldering end had dropped on to his leg until he smelt burning and felt the pain.

Nur watched with silent interest. Being opposite the Chief, he could not see the name that had so aroused and startled him, but he gauged it to be in the middle of the list.

Biodun caught Nur's eyes on him and growled to hide his embarrassment. He angrily swept away the ashes from the cigar that had fallen on the polished desk. 'Well, what are you going to do about it?' he managed to ask, his breath heavy and his forehead sweaty. In vain he tried to hide his shaking fingers from Nur by continuously tapping on the desk.

'This has at least pinpointed our area of investigation.'

'That is, if we resort to taking chances.'

'But we have to, Sir. What we should do now is to have these areas watched. It is the only thing we can do now.'

'Where do you imagine we can get enough people to cover all these places?' the Chief asked, running a finger down the list.

'I know how to do it, Sir, and even though we have only a limited staff, I think we should try.'

The Chief looked at him sourly for a few seconds, then pushed the list back towards him across the desk. As a gesture of dismissal, he selected another cigar from a tin and lit it.

The Inspector recognised the signal and left.

Back in his office, Nur neatly circled three names on the list with a pencil. The three names were in the middle of the list—the area that the Chief had gaped at:

125A Babolola Estate
209 The Amoto People's Church
262B Mr. Bola's residence

His curious mind wondered which of them could be the location of the mysterious secret society. He made up his mind to start investigation by concentrating on these three areas alone.

Secretly, he wondered about the Chief too. Since it was apparent that the Chief did not like this investigation, surely he could have stopped him if he wished? But, for reasons best known to himself, the Chief was acting in a very strange way, neither encouraging nor discouraging Nur's enquiries.

Nur glanced at his watch. It was getting near to six. He remembered the vow he had made earlier in the morning not to spend so much time at the office, and his promise to take his wife down to the beach.

This was a nice way of spending a weekend, he thought and grinned. He dialled a number on his internal telephone and summoned some of the policemen into his office. He despatched them to keep a strict surveillance on the areas he had selected at the beach.

Afterwards he telephoned his wife and was full of regret about not being able to take her out after all.

Chapter 6

The Kano-Lagos plane touched down at the Murtala
Muhammed International Airport, Lagos, at exactly 6.30 p.m. It sped along the runway, turned to the
left and stopped, the roaring of its engines slowly
dying out. Its doors opened and the passengers
began to descend the steps, some gazing astonished
at the intricate lights of the new airport.

Mansir stepped down, looked to the right and
then left and walked quickly to the large and airy
reception lobby of the airport. He looked afraid and
uncertain, and appeared to have put on some weight,
making the striped shirt he wore seem tight. He was
alone.

He sat down in the reception lobby, glanced through
a fashion magazine, got irritated and went over to
the bar where he ordered a shot of whisky. He
perched himself on a high stool in the crowded bar
and began to sip his drink.

At the Yankari Game Reserve, he had lied to his
wife, saying he would be going to Kofir in Kano
State to see Daudu's parents and tell them about
the unfortunate and untimely death of their son. His
wife had insisted that she too followed him, as she
had never been that far up in the North before. But
Mansir had made excuses which had sounded funny
and foolish even to him, and he had gone on alone

afterwards. So here he was now, at the Murtala Muhammed International Airport bar, sipping whisky and listening vaguely to the cries and laughter of the people in the bar, and the soft music filtering through the big loudspeakers of a stereo set. He turned over in his mind what the Black Temple would be deliberating on during its proposed meeting at two o'clock that morning. He no longer believed in or admired the Black Temple as he had before. He was now afraid of the organisation, for it had proved to be something mysterious and unknown. After all, it was the Temple that was ruining him by making him into a cold-blooded murderer and breaking up his home. The short holiday had done very little to raise the spirits of his wife, in spite of all that he hoped would come of it. But the material benefit was there to be considered. In few businesses could one make up to two thousand naira in a fortnight. If he were to leave the Black Temple, what would he do to earn such a good living, one which would finance the expensive tastes he had acquired? Nothing, he told himself. And he would become a nothing, like his father, and perhaps die a nothing as well. His children would have no prospects of becoming anything either. For in Nigeria, when you have money, you are something, and if you don't have it, you are nothing; even your own relatives will run away from you.

Mansir sipped more of his whisky. He was so engrossed in his own thoughts that he failed to notice a man sitting directly opposite him, reading a paper. The man occasionally glanced in his direction. He was small, and there was something frightening and menacing about his face—he had a scar running from his right eye, down by his temple and yet down again.

'Please, is there a telephone anywhere in here?' Mansir asked a waiter who was passing by, a tray of drinks delicately and yet professionally balanced on the palm of his hand. The waiter stopped and turned on his professional smile.

'We do have a phone of course, sir. If you go over to that counter, you will find there's a commercial one there.' He smiled again and left.

Mansir walked over to the counter a few metres away. He was surprisingly steady on his feet, and his head, as he walked, was thrust forward as usual.

He inserted a few coins and lifted the receiver. He looked about the bar vaguely as he waited for the telephone operator to connect him with Ibiang's residence. He again failed to notice the small man who had moved closer and settled himself in a chair, his face covered by the paper.

'Is that you, Ibiang?' Mansir spoke hoarsely into the mouthpiece.

'Yes. Please, who's that?'

'It's me, Mansir.'

'Oh Mansir! When did you return?'

'I've just returned today. I'm not calling from home. I'm still at the airport.'

There was a pause. Then Ibiang asked, 'Mansir, why did you go off like that?' There was a new sense of urgency in his voice.

'I had to, Ibiang.'

'What do you mean, you had to?'

'I repeat, I had to. It was because of my wife. She was taking things pretty badly. It should be obvious that I didn't want my home to break up. So we flew to Kano and from there to Bauchi State for a short holiday at the Yankari Game Reserve. But I have come back alone.'

'I hope you didn't tell her...' There was a note of menace in Ibiang's voice.

'For God's sake, why should I? She'd only be seeing me in a new image if I did.'

'That's alright then. Of course, I'm sure you always remember your oath. But you shouldn't have gone off like that. Suppose they had suspected you?'

'I couldn't help it. I said so.' Mansir looked around him. No one seemed to be within earshot. 'About the police... have they found anything yet?'

'No, nothing. But somehow they've managed to find out about our location—The Amoto People's Church. They seem to be taking an interest in it.'

Mansir took a deep breath. 'Then they've found something.'

'No. As I said, nothing yet. That Inspector Nur is too damned nosy. He's the only inquisitive one. He doesn't know what he's playing with, otherwise he would have laid off long ago. Perhaps it is his own death warrant he is signing. No one can change destiny.' How indifferently he spoke of death!

'The meeting,' Mansir began. 'I think it's due to begin at 2 a.m., isn't it?'

'Yes, the time has not changed. But the venue has. The meeting will now take place at the Bakawa Cemetery, Lagos Mainland.'

'Why's that, for God's sake?'

'Well, they decided it that way. It seemed sensible in view of the police interest.'

'Okay, Ibiang. Thank you and goodbye. I'll be coming over around 9.00 p.m.'

'Just a minute. Where are you staying?'

'At my flat, at a hotel. Somewhere. I don't know yet.'

'Take my advice and stay at your flat,' Ibiang said warningly, and hung up.

Mansir replaced the receiver. Why should he spend his money at a hotel anyway when he had his own flat? He was puzzled for a moment, then put the matter out of his mind.

He left the airport soon afterwards and took a taxi home.

The small man with the newspaper ran to the airport's parking lot, got into his car and followed in pursuit.

He was worried because he had not had time to telephone the Father.

By the time Mansir got to his flat it was nearly eight. The flat was dark and its front garden visibly untidy in spite of the darkness. The gleam of light from a nearby flat was comforting, driving away fears, real or imaginary. As he inserted his key into the lock, for the first time he had an uneasy feeling that he was being watched. He could feel eyes on him as he breathed, as he moved. He stood still listening to the cries of insects, the flapping of wings as bats wrestled with one another for a perch on the tall tree outside. He suddenly swung around, expecting to find a man crouching by a shrub or behind a tree.

There was no one. Only the long shadows greeted him. In his fear, he fancied he could hear his name being called. The voice sounded like Daudu's.

Hurriedly he stepped into the sitting room and put on the light. At once his eyes were attracted to a piece of paper on the dusty floor. He picked it up and read the neatly typed writing: MEETING TWO A.M. VENUE CHANGED TO BAKAWA CEMETERY, LAGOS MAINLAND. TURN BACK FOR DIRECTIONS.

BT

What would have happened if he had brought his wife along? She would have read the paper and would have known that her husband was a member of a secret society. The Black Temple was taking hazardous risks. If only he could find a profitable business... Mansir felt hot and cold at the same time, with a mixture of relief and fear.

The feeling of being watched persisted. He went into the bedroom where the pictures of Susanna and Shamsiddeen smiled down at him from the wall. He drew out a heavy box from under the bed and opened it. It contained things of his and Susanna's neatly folded inside. The box had a false bottom which his wife did not know of. He pressed a concealed button and turned the box over. The other side opened. Inside was a folded dark gown of about knee length with a couple of artificial cowrie shells fastened to it, two long and unusually thick candles, and a tin wrapped securely in a piece of cloth.

He took everything out and deposited them on the bed. They were the objects of the ritual. They had to be handy for the time of the meeting.

He closed the box and pushed it back under the bed, then he went to sit down in the sitting room. The flat was unusually silent and he wished there was a bottle of whisky to keep him company. He turned on the television set and hastily switched it off. As a last resort, he lit a cigarette with fingers that trembled strangely and, in his mind, went over his programme for tonight.

At 9.00 p.m. he would have to go and see Ibiang.

At 2.00 a.m. he would be on his way to the Bakawa Cemetery, Lagos Mainland.

He tried to keep the feeling of unease that he felt within under control. It was useless.

The headlights of Mansir's car at last picked up the small signpost by the roadside on which was written: THE BAKAWA CEMETERY—there was a short arrow to show the way. Mansir sighed, more out of fear than relief, braked and drove the car bumpily along the narrow, untarred road leading up to the cemetery. He parked by a clump of bushes where the car would not be seen too easily.

It was very quiet. The whole of Lagos, that city of daytime bustle, seemed to be asleep.

He was dressed in a black gown and had a cloak pulled up to his face to hide his identity. He carried with him a piece of candle, a box of matches and a small tin. He walked along the wet, narrow path leading to the cemetery. The night was so dark and chilly that he had difficulty groping for his way. On either side of the path were tall, dark trees, their dense branches and leaves housing the noisy bats that added to the sinister feeling of the place.

His heart full of fear, the hairs on his neck erect, Mansir walked on until he, too, became part of the darkness. The atmosphere reminded him of a horror film he had watched together with his wife about a year ago. The film had been so frightening that if it had not been for her he would have gone out of the cinema theatre. But he stayed because he had to pretend a show of manliness.

He saw a candle light flickering away in the distance. It was at the foot of a big cross, whose shadow stretched out lengthily. Suddenly there were more candle lights and Mansir could see the vague outlines of men standing near a grave. Mansir knew then that he must be a bit late.

He joined the group of men, but he couldn't identify any of them. They all stood silently, each one holding a lighted candle, each one dressed alike in a black gown with the cloak pulled up to his face. He pushed his way through them to the candle on the grave. There he lighted his own and stepped back, waiting expectantly.

'You are late,' said a tall figure in a sombre tone. Mansir recognised the Father's voice.

'I'm sorry. It was due to my car. It wouldn't start,' he lied, in a voice that sounded almost as though it did not belong to him.

The Father pulled down his cloak, revealing his thin face and went over to the grave. 'We called this meeting today,' he began, 'so that you may all come and show evidence of your sacrifices. We shouldn't waste too much time, I believe, as we all have something to do.'

There were about ten men there, standing beside the Father. Presently, one of them came forward and deposited a tin on the grave, stepped back and said: 'Father, the heart and the blood are in there. As long as I live I shall strive to do the duties given to me by the Black Temple. My loyalty will never be in question.'

The Father nodded silently.

The Father is the pastor of death, Mansir thought, as he made his way to the grave where he also placed a tin and repeated what the first man had said. He stepped back, the gentle wind fanning his gown and occasionally threatening to snuff out the light of his candle.

The Father knelt down and inspected the tins, seemed satisfied with what he saw and stood erect again.

'As long as we have faith and are loyal to the Black Temple,' he began, 'the benefits that flow therefrom shall never cease. I must speak to you about the police... there's nothing to be afraid of. If members of the Black Temple find it almost impossible to expose or even know a lot of each other, how can the police ever hope to discover anything? Do not forget our powers, our influence and our wide membership. Just continue with your work as usual. Thank you and goodnight.'

Back at his flat, Mansir began to explore new possibilities of starting afresh in life, of getting himself into a promising business venture. He had some ₦12,000 in his account and he also owned a 50% share in a small restaurant at No. 36, Lamido Street, Lagos Mainland. No one knew about the restaurant but himself and his partner, who supervised the business. He had not told his wife because he did not want her, as was usual with her, to be continually asking him questions, like how and where had he got the money for the restaurant. He had not told Ibiang either, because he did not want anything to leak out to the Black Temple.

It was because of his foresight that he had become a partner in the restaurant. He knew that one's membership of a secret society was often unpredictable and uncertain. He had imagined himself being kicked out of the organisation for some mistake he might commit or because he no longer wanted to be a member. He had therefore bought a part of the business to have something to fall back on in case anything unforseen should happen.

His only worry was that the money from the restaurant could not support his lavish spending. He considered investing more money so that they could turn the restaurant into a first class, more luxurious one, and his heart leapt with hope. With more money and Susanna, his partner and himself to look after it, he knew the restaurant would be a success.

Then after the preparations were completed, he would give his notice of withdrawal from the Black Temple and lead an honest life. He didn't know, however, when the picture of the mutilated body of Daudu would stop haunting his mind. Nor when he would stop regarding himself as a murderer.

The following morning he called a taxi and went to the airport to book a plane to the North so that he could continue holidaying with his family for two more days. He felt that perhaps he would discuss the new business in detail there.

What Mansir didn't know, however, was that membership of the Black Temple was permanent. A withdrawal after the initiation amounted to betrayal.

Chapter 7

The Father, the pastor of the Amoto People's Church and chief organiser of the Black Temple, dressed in an ankle-length kaftan without a cap, let the motor boat he was driving circle lazily in the sea, dancing to the tunes of the waves and the wind. He considered the squat, thickset man sitting beside him.

They had left the beach far away behind them but could just make out the outlines of people bathing in the distance.

It was a hobby of the Father's to take a boat to sea as a way of relieving himself of his heavy duties. Today, however, he was mixing business with pleasure.

The short, thickset man became aware of the Father's eyes on him and shifted uneasily.

'I'm listening,' he said weakly, staring blankly at the open sea.

'When did you last do a job for us?'

'Two weeks ago. Perhaps three.' The man was uncertain.

'You are going to do another job today. It's a very simple one, though.' The Father regarded him again. 'As you're so good with cars, I'm sure you wouldn't find it very difficult to stage an accident.'

The short man grinned suddenly. So he had done nothing wrong after all. Too bad he had had to suffer all that worry when he had been told that the Father wanted him.

The Father continued. 'You will take the Dodge. It's a strong heavy car. If, however, you fail to stage an accident, this might come in handy.'

The Father opened the glove compartment of the motor boat and took out a .38 police special. The gun was new and loaded. He handed the gun to the short man who inspected it with loving eyes.

'Yes, it might well come in handy.' The short man was becoming more and more animated. 'But I really can't see why I should fail to stage an accident, though. Hey, this piece is really beautiful.' He frowned suddenly. 'Who is it to be?' he asked, after a pause.

A slow smile stretched the Father's tight-lipped mouth. He nodded gently and smiled with confidence at the man beside him.

'Inspector Nur of the Linivia Island Police,' he said in a soft voice. 'But be careful—the guy is very smart.'

Meanwhile, back at his office, Nur was beginning to lose hope in the success of his investigations. The men he had stationed along the beach were yet to report anything worthwhile. Everything was going on as usual.

The case was beginning to irritate him but he knew that he must be patient. He was dealing with a clever and well-organised secret society which could be very dangerous.

Irritably, he glanced at his wrist watch, which showed 3.16 p.m., and then glanced enviously at the two other inspectors with whom he shared the office. Both of them were concentrating on their own work. Nur felt that he had not much to concentrate on and this worried him.

He put on his peaked cap and stood up.

'I'm going home, Inspector Hassan. If something turns up you know where to find me.'

Hassan looked up from his work. 'You're a bit in front of yourself these days, aren't you?' He glanced at his wrist watch. 'Why it is not yet 3.30. That is when your shift ends, damn you.'

The other inspector, a young man in his late twenties, looked up, smiled at Nur and busied himself once more with his work.

'Well, you can put on a front for me,' Nur told Hassan.

Hassan laughed. 'When the Chief doesn't care any more about who does what here, I don't think it matters all that much.'

Nur raised a hand in agreement and left.

He picked up his car and drove it out into the traffic. The traffic was unusually heavy at this time of the day because this was the time most ministries closed and all the workers left for home.

As he followed his usual way home, Nur became aware of a Dodge following closely behind him. There was only one car between them.

Unexpectedly, there was a break in the traffic and Nur increased speed. He turned right at a T-junction and drove along the Bombi road. Glancing in the rearview mirror, he saw that the Dodge had taken the same turning and had caught up with him.

He was suddenly alerted. The Dodge could possibly be tailing him. He tried to make out the outline of the driver but failed. But he carefully memorised the plate number of the Dodge—TT132 R.

To make certain if the Dodge was really tailing him, he swung his car along a narrow, deserted road that led to a small industrial block, some five kilometres away. He increased speed and glanced in the rearview mirror again.

The Dodge made the same turn, then suddenly began surging forward with unexpected speed, making straight for Nur's car.

Nur braked, and made as if to turn right, then all of a sudden turned left. Tyres screeched and the car went bumping along the uneven ground off the road. He had narrowly escaped a crash.

The Dodge sped past, made a U-turn and roared towards Nur again. Nur reversed just in time to avoid a head-on collision, edged the car onto the road and quickly swerved to the right. The Dodge caught Nur's car on the side. Nur heard a 'bang' and felt the car swerve off the road out of control.

For a moment he thought the car was going to turn over. But it only skidded for about two metres and then stopped.

The Dodge reversed, drove ahead and stopped. Suddenly several gun shots cracked out into the still air.

Nur crouched down in his seat, then slowly opened the door, shielding his face with one hand from the windscreen that had been shattered as bullets rained on it. Glass seemed to be flying everywhere.

Just then a truck could be seen approaching from the direction of the industrial block and the shooting stopped abruptly. Gazing just above the level of the window, Nur saw the Dodge speed away.

He hastily slid back under the steering wheel and turned the ignition key. The car refused to start. He tried again, shook his head sadly and came out to assess the extent of the damage.

The car was practically a ruin—one side was completely pushed in and the windscreen was shattered.

'Are you in any trouble, Sir?' the wide-eyed driver of the truck called out. He had pulled up at the side of the road.

Nur went over to him. 'My car wouldn't start...'

'There's been a shooting—armed robbers, am I wrong?'

Nur ignored the question. 'You're very busy? Could you tow me to the Linivia Police Compound?'

The driver considered this, then looked at Nur who was in his uniform.

'You help me, I help you,' the driver began. 'That's how the world should be. Let's go over to the car and see what we can do.'

A few minutes later the car was being towed to the Linivia Island Police Compound.

Someone wanted Nur dead. But who could it be, he wondered? It must have something to do with the affair of the secret society, he thought. He had probably stepped on something concrete, but without fully knowing what. He told himself he would have to be very cautious in the future. It was unfortunate that the driver of the Dodge had got away, otherwise it might have been his first major break into the 'mysterious murders'.

When Nur told his wife about the 'accident' and let her inspect the car, the young woman burst into uncontrollable sobs.

'Come on dear, don't act like a child. After all I'm here—alive.' He took her in his arms but Lami continued to sob.

'You don't know how I feel,' she said between sobs. 'Leave this case, Nur!' she pleaded. 'They are determined to kill you and they'll surely succeed if you don't lay off! For my sake, please?'

'Everyone has his time of death, Lami. It is predestined, as you know and believe very well. So stop worrying yourself. No one can kill me before my time.'

He patted her bottom gently to reassure her and then led her to an armchair in the small sitting room.

'The Chief of Police telephoned twice. He didn't leave any message though,' Lami said, wiping away the tears on her face with a handkerchief.

'I'll meet him tomorrow,' Nur tried to keep the anxiety out of his voice. He went over to the telephone and dialled some numbers. 'Is that Hamis?' he asked into the mouthpiece.

There was a short pause, then a voice cracked through. 'Yes. Who's that?'

Hamis was Nur's friend in the Motor Vehicle Registration Department. Nur identified himself and they greeted each other.

'You are damned lucky to get me,' Hamis began. 'It's after four now. We have too much work in the office today, so I'm working late. What is it, Nur?'

'Please, I want to know the owner of a white Dodge with the plate number TT132R.' Nur had written the number in his book to make sure that he would not forget it.

Sitting in the armchair, Lami glanced sharply at Nur—Nur grinned at her.

'A hit and run case?' Hamis was asking.

'No. But there's something cooking—I can't say over the phone.'

'Okay. Hold on for a minute while I look it up.'

There was a short delay followed by a rustling of papers.

'You still there, Nur?' Hamis was back on the line.

'Of course.'

'The Dodge belongs to the Amoto People's Church.'

Nur's heart missed a beat.

'Did you say the Amoto People's Church?' Nur tried to keep his voice steady.

'That's right.'

'Well, thank you very much, Hamis. Meet you some time or other at the club.'

Hamis said goodbye and hung up.

Hastily Nur dialled some numbers on the phone again. He could almost hear his heart beating against his chest.

'Is Sergeant Andrews at home?'

'Yes, but he's having a shower,' a woman's voice answered. There was the faint cry of a child in the background. 'Oh, just a moment,' the woman continued, 'here he is.'

'Who is it?' Andrews asked.

'Inspector Nur. Do you have the Land Rover with you?' Nur almost shouted in his excitement.

'Yes, Sir. Anything wrong?'

'For God's sake, don't just stand there. Hurry up and come and collect me from my home!'

'Yes, Sir!'

Nur dropped the receiver back on its rest.

'Where are you going now?' Lami asked.

'To the police station. I'm going to alert our men about the Dodge.'

Minutes later, Andrews arrived and they drove off to the Linivia Island Police Headquarters. On their way Nur told Andy everything.

At his office, which was empty as the other inspectors had gone home, Nur called a meeting of the senior police officers. Briefly he explained the situation to them, pointing out his suspicions and his hopes.

'So you see,' he concluded, 'we are up against one of the toughest, most violent criminal organisations in Lagos.'

He stood up and went over to the large map on the wall. About seven pairs of eyes followed him.

'I'm now certain that there is a connection between the secret society that we are trying to trace and the Amoto People's Church. I think the Church could be the location of the secret society—'

'The Church, sir?' a baffled police officer asked.

'Yes, the Church could merely be a front for the society's hideous activities.'

He pointed at a dot on the map. 'That's where the Church is. What we must do is concentrate all of our attention here.' He circled the dot with a red marker. 'But we must be careful. They are really dangerous. They tried to kill me with a Dodge today.'

'Ah, excuse me, Sir,' a sergeant cut in. 'Did you say a Dodge,' he asked.

'Yes. What's the matter?'

'Could it have the following plate number?' He produced a paper from his breast pocket. 'TT132R?'

Nur leaned forward. 'How—?'

'It was reported stolen about two hours ago by the pastor of the Amoto People's Church.'

'The bastards!' Nur cried. 'They're trying to build up an alibi. Well, anyway, let's just concentrate on the Church. When the right time comes I'll get us a search warrant. One word of caution here.' He paused. 'Do not listen to the Chief. I know that's against discipline, but the Chief has recently started to act in a way a policeman should be ashamed of. For reasons best known to himself he is trying to discourage this investigation. Have I made myself clear?'

The officers hesitated for a while, looked at one another in surprise, then nodded gravely.

Nur sat back in his chair and smiled to himself. At least he had the officers behind him.

It was now only a matter of waiting for something to turn up.

Something always does.

Chapter 8

Mansir and his family returned to Lagos as they had planned. The last part of the holiday had been especially happy. This was due to the fact that Mansir had told his wife about his plan to pull out of the Black Temple and set himself up in a legitimate business. Mansir was particularly happy because Susanna seemed to have forgiven him, despite the fact that he had told her in detail about the murder he had committed. It was something for which he could hardly forgive himself. At times he wondered whether it could really have been him. Only an un-calculating zombie could have done such a terrible thing.

Their only problem now was to make sure that Mansir pulled safely out of the deadly organisation. Susanna had tried to reason with him while at the Yankari Game Reserve that pulling out of the Black Temple might present problems, for such organisations didn't usually want deserters to go about exposing their deadly secrets.

It took about two hours to clean the dusty flat thoroughly. Afterwards the family sat in the sitting room talking business and gazing at the scene around them. The curtains had been pulled aside and from where he sat Mansir could see, through the window, the whole extent of the small river with the dead end. The level of the water had risen considerably. Rays from the evening sun filtered through the glass, making beautiful patterns on the neat carpet.

Mansir reached for the telephone.

'Who are you going to call?' Susanna asked him, forcing Shamsiddeen, who wanted to play with a glass of water, on to her knees.

'Ibiang,' answered Mansir. 'I must seek professional advice from him. He should know the right channels for me to follow.'

'To think that he talked you into all this mess,' she said bitterly.

'I was young and inexperienced then. I was just an ordinary villager. I bear no hard feelings towards him, though, for had it not been for him, I wouldn't have met you. Then life would really have been incomplete,' he grinned.

'Well you could certainly say that,' she grinned back.

Mansir dialled Ibiang's number and listened to the burr-burr of the phone. There was no answer. Thinking that he might have made a mistake, he dialled the number again. But there was still no answer. Perhaps there was no one in the house.

He replaced the receiver.

'He's not there?' his wife asked.

'No one seems to be in the house. But that is rather strange. If Ibiang is out, Marian ought to be in. They hardly ever go out together. Thieves are very active these days.'

He sat quietly for a while, deep in thought.

'I think I will go and check up, or perhaps wait for him at his house. In the meantime, prepare yourself

as if you're going out shopping and go down to
restaurant. To see this problem through, we m
not take any chances. While you're at th
restaurant, check and see that everything is in
order—particularly the accounts book. I'll write a
note for you to take to the manager.' Mansir tore a
sheet of paper from a writing pad on the TV set and
wrote the note.

'Discuss the details of the new investment with
him, okay?' he said.

Susana nodded and pocketed the note.

'Good. Till we meet then.'

As he rose to go, Shamsiddeen stretched his small
arms towards Mansir, wanting his father to pick
him up. Mansir only patted him on the stomach and
then hurried out of the flat before the child began to
cry.

Shortly afterwards, Susanna finished her preparations and, locking the door of the flat carefully, left,
carrying a shopping bag in one hand.

Mansir drove through the decorated gate of the
Amont Estate. The well-kept lawns, the magnificent
buildings and swimming pools fascinated him, as
they had always done. He drove along the narrow,
tarred road and pulled up by Ibiang's house.

He hoped Ibiang would have returned by now.
Before knocking on the door he checked for Ibiang's
car in the garage. The Volvo 244 DL that Ibiang had
bought about a year and a half before was there all
right.

With relief showing in his face, he went to the door
and knocked. He could hear the sound echoing in-

side, but no one answered. He knocked again and waited for about a minute. Still no one answered.

Gently, he turned the handle of the door. To his surprise, the door swung inwards. This was very strange, he told himself.

Curious, but a little afraid, he stepped into the giant sitting room and called out Ibiang's name. Silence answered him. Glancing without interest at the empty bottles of whisky on a small table and the dust that had started to collect on top of the TV set, he went into Ibiang's bedroom, to make sure that Ibiang wasn't fast asleep.

The bed was empty. The bedsheets were crumpled and the floor was dusty. Something sticking out from beneath the pillow attracted his attention. He lifted the pillow to see what it was.

It was a small .25 gun.

He left the gun as he had found it and went out of the bedroom and entered Marian's bedroom.

There was no one inside there either, but there was a dark patch staining the rug on the floor. Mansir knelt to see what it was and felt a creepy sensation run up his spine.

What he saw was dried blood.

Hurriedly he came out of the house and closed the front door. Just then a neighbour came towards him. She was an Indian.

'Are you looking for Mr Ibiang?' she asked.

'Yes, but no one seems to be around,' Mansir answered in a husky voice.

'Mr Ibiang is not well. He's at the Lagos University Teaching Hospital.'

'Hospital? What's wrong with him?'

'I don't know.'

'Well, thank you very much.' Mansir went back quickly to his car and drove off.

At the Lagos University Teaching Hospital, Mansir managed to locate Ibiang in the emergency ward. Ibiang could scarcely speak and his thick upper lip quivered with nervousness. His legs were swollen, and Mansir knew that this indicated a heart problem.

Mansir sat down beside him. 'Ibiang... whatever is the matter...?'

Ibiang's eyes seemed to glaze over and for the moment Mansir thought the man was going to faint. Then slowly Ibiang tapped at his chest with his hand.

'Heart problem... hypertension and so on, they say,' he croaked.

'Where is Marian?'

Ibiang suddenly began to cough and a nurse had to come to attend to him. She warned Mansir that he could have only two minutes more with Ibiang and would then have to leave. Ibiang was very sick.

'They wanted me to sacrifice her,' Ibiang whispered. 'But I gave her some money and told her to go away and live somewhere up north.'

Mansir knew that Ibiang was lying to him. If not, how could he explain the dried blood he had seen? To think that a man could kill his own niece for money!

He looked down at the crumpled figure but could feel no sympathy for Ibiang. He leaned down to him and said, 'Had it not been for you I wouldn't be in this mess now. But I'm pulling out of the Black Temple for good.'

Ibiang looked at him and shuddered. He mumbled something like 'Impossible' and started to cough again. The nurse returned, looking stern. Mansir's time was up.

Mansir scarcely looked back at Ibiang as he walked to the door.

Susanna came back earlier than Mansir. She was very enthusiastic about the restaurant. It was well-built and in a strategic position; the kitchen equipment was modern and, why, even the dining tables were modern!

The manager had also been enthusiastic. Why, the three of them could make the small restaurant compete with the Bristol Hotel, if they really worked hard.

'Why are you so quiet?' Susanna asked when Mansir didn't share her enthusiasm.

He told her about Ibiang and about Marian's disappearance and outlined his suspicions—'I can't ... I can't forgive myself for killing Daudu...'

Susanna snuggled up to him, comforting him. 'It wasn't your fault, Mansir. You were conditioned to behave like a machine.'

Chapter 9

The day and the time had been fixed and Mansir intended to withdraw from the Black Temple this very day.

'Good luck,' Susanna whispered as she escorted him to the door.

Mansir mumbled something and nearly stumbled as he walked down the five steps outside his flat. What would he tell the Father? Would the Black Temple allow him to withdraw willingly? He shuddered at these questions, questions that could determine the course of his life. He turned back to see Susanna looking encouragingly at him.

'Go on, Mansir. After all it is not a question of life and death. Just tell them clearly that you're pulling out. I wish I could come with you.' She smiled sweetly at him.

Mansir nodded. 'But you can't come with me,' he warned, walking to his car. As he drove away, Susanna waved at him from the doorway.

The morning traffic was heavy and, as he drove in it, Mansir kept looking enviously at the people in other cars and the pedestrians by the roadside. Most of these people were innocent and did not have many problems—unlike him. He wished he was one of these passers-by.

At exactly 9.30 a.m. he saw the signboard on

which was written: The Amoto People's Church. His palms were wet with sweat and his heart raw with a mixed feeling of fear and curiosity. He pulled his car up in the parking lot and walked towards the door.

Several metres away, plain-clothes detectives from the Linivia Island Police watched without much interest. They were used to seeing people coming in and going out of the church.

There was no one inside the dimly-lit church. Heavy blinds were used to keep sunlight out. Mansir walked to the next door, paused, took off his shoes and knocked.

A heavily-built man with a rifle strapped to his arm opened the door. He beckoned and then, scarcely looking at Mansir, closed the door and locked it behind him.

'Where do I find the Father?' Mansir asked him.

'Down at the hall.'

Mansir walked along the short, narrow corridor that led to the hall a little way ahead. When he reached the door, he knocked and waited. He could hear the sound of the sea faintly as the powerful waves lapped against the shore. The distant cries of excited bathers came to his ears.

The Father himself, dressed in black, opened the door. He led the way towards the big hall that contained paintings of the solar system and many strange creatures. The hall had several doors to rooms that Mansir had never entered, holding things that he had never seen. When they reached a small room, the Father motioned to Mansir and they sat down opposite each other.

'What have you come for?' the Father asked, in that authoritative voice. His penetrating gaze seemed to search Mansir all over.

Mansir looked away and shifted uneasily. Why were the words he had rehearsed so often now about to fail him?

'Father, I've served the Black Temple honestly and efficiently...'

'Oh yes, I know.'

'I've risked my life and freedom very often in the past to smuggle goods either out of or into the Nigerian borders.'

'That's also right. But what do you want me to say?' The Father glanced at his watch. 'I'm a very busy man, you know. I've some men to attend to and time is against me, as usual.'

'Oh yes, I know. I'll try to make it brief.' Mansir shifted in his seat again. His palms were wet and his heart was hammering. 'I even killed for you.'

'For the Black Temple, you mean.'

'Yes, for the Black Temple, sorry.' He sighed and shook his head regretfully.

'I'm still listening,' the Father said impatiently.

'Father, I don't want... I want to renounce my membership.'

The Father stiffened and there was a painful silence.

'Why don't you want to work with us any more?' the Father asked, when he got over his apparent shock and disbelief. To think they had been planning to give Mansir a senior post, he thought in astonishment.

Now that he had said it, the words came more easily to Mansir. 'It's just that I'm tired. I mean, a man has a right to do what he wants with his life. Don't I have the right to start a decent life?'

'Meaning we lead an inhuman life? You're still a boy. No more than a mere schoolkid.' The Father leaned forward and stared at Mansir's sweaty forehead. 'Doesn't the Temple pay well? Don't you remember how you came to this city? Are you not grateful for what the Temple has done for you?' He sounded scornful.

Mansir shook his head silently. 'I didn't say I was not grateful to the Temple for what it has done for me. After all, I came to this city a poor and dejected man. I am grateful, Father, but I still want to pull out.'

The Father sat back. 'Of course a man has the right to do as he wants with his life—that is, of course, if he is not under a bond.'

Mansir stared at the Father without answering. The Father was cool and composed—the Father who was the pastor of crime and death, the link between the two invisibles of the underworld and the criminals of the real world.

'But I'm not under a bond.'

'You are. Do you not remember your oath?'

'But it didn't say that I must remain a member all my life. All it said was that I must be loyal to the Black Temple and must not betray it all my life.'

'Yes, I know. I should know the oath better than you. But what guarantee do we have that you won't tell anyone anything about us if or when you cease to be a member?'

Mansir looked down at the table between them and then raised his eyes to stare high above at the small window. He realised that his fingers were not steady.

'I have always been loyal. Won't you take my

word if I say I won't tell anyone anything?'

What about all the strange powers they claimed, Mansir thought? He had told his wife about the Black Temple, and yet the Father seemed ignorant of it. Could the Temple have been bluffing?

Suddenly, the Father smiled. It was a cruel smile, the type that neither reached the heart nor the eyes.

'We can take your word, Mansir, if you promise not to open your mouth to anybody.'

Mansir grabbed at the Father's knees. 'Is it settled then?' he asked, looking hopefully at the Father. 'I promise no one will ever know about it—.'

The Father pushed Mansir's hands away gently. 'Yes, it is settled, but on one condition. This condition applies to all members who intend to renounce their memberships.'

'What is the condition?'

'It is simple and easy to fulfil.' The Father looked hard at Mansir and repeated, 'Yes, easy to fulfil. It is simply that a member seeking to renounce his membership must hand back to the Black Temple all that he acquired during his membership.'

Mansir was calculating quickly in his mind. He had almost ₦12,000 in his account, his two-bedroom flat and a 50% share in a restaurant. He decided not to disclose his share in the restaurant since it was what he and his family were hoping to fall back upon.

'I should say I have about ₦12,000 in my bank, the flat and, of course, the car.'

'You have much more than that,' the Father stated.

'Which I'm not aware of?'

The Father ignored the mockery. 'No, you are

very much aware of it. When you first came to Lagos you were a bachelor, is that not right?'

A sudden fear swept over Mansir. What was the Father trying to say?

'Yes, that's right,' he answered weakly.

'So, if my calculations are correct, you have acquired a family—a wife and a son—during your association with us?'

'Yes, but what has that—?'

'The condition says "A member must give back all that he acquires during his association with the Black Temple." If, therefore, you want to pull out, you must hand back the money in your possession, your flat, your car and last but not least, your family. Without us, you wouldn't have any of these.'

Mansir stared at the Father the way a man would stare at a snake, concealing none of his hatred for him. Then abruptly he stood up, only to sit down again. He was feeling very weak. There was sweat in his belly and under his arms. His head was suddenly hot with pain and his legs felt like rubber.

'You are not human!' he yelled at last, banging his fist on the table. 'You want me to surrender my family to you and go about in the world like a wandering Jew? Are you never tired of killing innocent people?'

'As I said before, I have some men to attend to and time is running against me. You asked me the condition and I told you. If you feel you can go through with it, then it is goodbye, but if you can't...' The Father's voice was icily calm.

Mansir was telling himself to play it cool. If he let himself become angry and let his thinking become confused, how could he hope to find a way out of this mess? He took a deep breath.

'Suppose I can't?' he asked, surprisingly calm.

'Then you can't renounce your membership.' The Father glanced at his watch again and stood up. 'Well?' he asked.

There was a plan already forming in Mansir's mind, a plan, he hoped, that would see him and his family through.

He stood up as well. 'Sorry for that outburst, Father. I guess I nearly went out of my mind. As I can't satisfy your condition, I once again pledge to be a loyal member of the Black Temple.' He hoped he was not too sudden in taking back the membership.

'That's all right, then,' the Father said. 'I will take your word not to betray us, otherwise... I shouldn't bore you with the consequences which you already know very well.' The Father left.

Mansir emerged from the Amoto People's Church and went back to his car. As he drove for a while he looked back to see if the Father had sent someone to follow him.

There was a blue Honda Civic trailing him. He increased speed and drove to Ibiang's house at the Amont Estate. There he took the .25 he had seen.

Now it had turned into a question of life and death, in spite of what Susanna had said.

As he drove back to his home, he didn't even bother to look back at the Honda Civic again.

Chapter 10

Susanna sprang to her feet and almost knocked Shamsiddeen aside as she rushed to the door when she heard Mansir's car. She had been extremely anxious about her husband and prayed for his success. Mansir climbed the stairs silently. His face was set and his eyes were red.

'It's bad news. Let's go inside, we can't talk here.' They went inside, closed the door and then sat down.

'Shall I bring you some water or something?' Susanna asked.

'No, nothing, thank you. Oh, Susanna! People are not human nowadays.'

Mansir told her all that had happened at the Temple, adding nothing and leaving nothing out.

When he had finished, he noticed that Susanna's eyes were cloudy as if she was likely to burst into tears. Shamsiddeen plodded towards him and he embraced the child with a new sense of warmth. Deep inside him he feared the pain of separation.

'We may escape from this mess, Susanna, but I don't think I can escape from the hands of the law. Whichever way I try to play my cards now, the Black Temple will surely make an attempt to kill me. What I don't want is to involve you in my trouble. So I've—'

Susanna interrupted him. 'Why can't we simply go away, Mansir, and settle somewhere else? We have some money and we can make a good start.'

'How simple you are, Susanna. If that had been possible, wouldn't I have suggested it myself? The Black Temple, my dear, right now is keeping a watch on me. One suspicious move from me and I'm dead.'

Susanna looked at him silently. She began to sob softly. He placed one hand on top of hers and squeezed. 'Don't cry any more and don't lose hope. As a singer once said, "Where there is life there is always hope." We may really escape, Susanna. Tomorrow is Sunday—I know what to do.'

Craddled in his father's arms, Shamsiddeen looked at his sobbing mother curiously.

The following morning, after a cold shower, Mansir began to outline to his wife his plans and programmes for the day.

'By 9.00 a.m. I know the Amoto People's Church will be almost full, as today is Sunday. Most of the people who go there are hypocrites. But some, as you know, are innocent.'

He munched a bean-cake (akara) and paused to swallow. 'That is the only opportunity I have of getting at the Father without raising any suspicion. The Father is a criminal on an international scale. He was once involved, so I have learned, with IN-TERPOL in connection with drug trafficking. And this same fast-calculating man is after me now. We, the Hausa, have a saying, "Kill your enemy before your enemy kills you." I want to put an end to the

Father before he gets me first.'

Susanna shuddered. 'Are you not complicating your case rather more? Oh, Mansir, why don't you simply tell the police? After all, it's only a matter of a telephone call...'

'The police can't find anything out that way. And they can't bring the Father to book. They have nothing personally against him. But I... I want to start something that will lead to the total destruction of the Black Temple. I can only do this by catching the Father unawares. Of course I'll tell the police something to keep them on the alert.' He looked at his watch. 'I will shortly be leaving here. What you must do is give me an hour's start after I have gone. After an hour, take a taxi to the Linivia Island Police compound. You know where it is, I take it?'

'Yes, but why?'

'The only way I can escape, if at all... is to keep in contact with the police. More than that I want the law, through me, to put a stop to the murderous activities of the Black Temple.'

He pushed away the plate of oats and drank a glass of milk. For someone who was about to be involved in an adventure, he was eating pretty happily and not doing badly.

He continued, looking keenly at his wife, 'When you reach there, ask for Inspector Nur's bungalow. You know the man, surely? The papers always give him wide publicity. He's the only one I trust in the Linivia Island Police because he's the only one that has shown keen interest in the activities of the Black Temple. Because of him, smuggled goods can't be brought in directly to the Temple by sea now. I wouldn't be surprised if they are planning to kill him as well. Now, in his bungalow, you'll meet his wife. Just say you are a guest and make yourself comfortable. That is the best way to protect yourself and the child from the murderous hands of the people of the Black Temple. I hope I'll meet you there.'

He rose, took the .25 out of his pocket and checked it. The gun was loaded. 'Is everything clear?' he asked.

Susanna nodded and got up hurriedly when she heard Shamsiddeen wailing from their bedroom. 'Shamsiddeen has woken up. I'll go and clean him.'

'No,' Mansir protested, pocketing the gun. 'I'll do that today.'

Susanna sat back and rested her head on her palms, overcome by emotion.

For the first time since Shamsiddeen was born, Mansir bathed the child clean. He was full of emotion himself. This might be the last time he would hold his son so close.

Around 9.00 a.m. Mansir was ready to leave. His wife escorted him to the car and made no effort to control the tears that were streaming down her face. Mansir's eyes were also clouded.

'In about an hour's time...'

Susanna nodded.

He drove away. After a few metres, he glanced in the rear view mirror. Susanna was still there, looking after him.

He edged the car out into the traffic and, after a while, looked back to see if the Honda Civic he had seen yesterday was still following him. There was only one car between him and the Honda Civic.

At a telephone booth by the roadside he stopped

to make a call. Through the glass door of the booth he saw the Honda Civic park some metres away.

'Please connect me with the Linivia Island Police,' he told the telephone operator.

There was a 'click' and he knew he had been connected.

'Is that Inspector Nur?' he asked.

'Linivia Island Police. Please, who's that?'

'I want to speak to Inspector Nur.'

'Please, who are you?'

'An informer with a lot of information.'

'About what?'

'The Black Temple.'

'What?'

'I mean the Amoto People's Church; the mysterious murders.'

'Okay. Hold on please.'

A new voice sounded. 'This is Inspector Nur.'

Carefully, lest he should omit something, Mansir told Nur all there was to know about the Black Temple—its underground rackets and connections, its location, the hidden smuggled goods, and so on. In conclusion, he lied, 'There's a large consignment of heroin coming in in about forty minutes' time. I would suggest that you raid the place then. By the way, my name is Mansir.'

He hung up, and hurried out of the booth to his car. If they had traced the call at all, they would be here any time from now. The best thing to do was to fly away.

He had deliberately lied about the heroin so as to give himself time to finish the job he had in hand at the Amoto People's Church.

He looked back. The Honda Civic was still

following closely behind him.

The parking lot of the Amoto People's Church was filled with cars, motorcycles and bicycles. Mansir managed to find a place away from the parking lot and parked the car in such a way that he wouldn't encounter any problems if he needed to get away in a hurry.

He went past the front door of the church and followed a narrow alley that led directly down to the sea. In the alley he stopped and hid behind a rock. He looked up in time to see the blue Honda Civic pull up and a small man open the door and start towards the alley.

He rose from his hiding place and walked down the alley, determined to get into the church through the back door.

As for the small man, he was in for a big surprise. The back door was open but there was a strong looking man guarding it. As he went through the door, the guard greeted Mansir.

Mansir went past two rooms, turned a corner and stopped. After a while, he heard the light steps of the small man trailing after him.

Just in case the small man was carrying a gun, Mansir took out his gun from his trouser pocket and waited, expectant.

The small man turned the corner, walking quite confidently. When he saw Mansir, he reeled back and his hand instinctively, yet professionally, went towards his pocket.

Mansir hit the man in the stomach. The small man doubled up and started to moan. Mansir pocketed the gun and raised the small man off his feet. Then he hit the man again with all of his strength. The man went suddenly limp.

Mansir listened for any sound. There was none. He caried the limp man over his shoulder to a half-opened door nearby. The key was still in the lock.

Inside the room it was dark and dusty. There were many empty cartons scattered about. He deposited the unconscious man in a corner and went out of the room, locking the door behind him and putting the key inside his breast pocket. Then he walked along the familiar way, past the hall where he had been in-itiated into the Black Temple, past the narrow cor-ridor. He stopped when he was about to enter the church from the back door. From the doorway he peeped into the church.

The heavy blinds had been pushed aside to allow a little sunlight in.

The people in the church were singing prayer songs loudly. The Father, in his usual role of the pastor, was standing in the pulpit before the big crucifix, singing with the people.

The hypocrite. The bastard, thought Mansir.

He withdrew the gun slowly from his pocket, his heart banging against his chest, his fingers itching to fire at the man who had become a demon and a monster in his eyes.

Sweat flowed from his forehead, down the bridge of his nose and on to his lips. Something was churn-ing in his stomach and the sound was, to him, as loud as a gun shot.

He looked back to make sure that no one was watching him, stepped forward, then suddenly stood still. The people had stopped singing. There was a heavy silence in the church.

Mansir peered at them again. The people were

praying silently, heads bent down and their eyes closed.

Mansir decided to grab the opportunity. Walking stealthily, he went into the church and stopped when he came directly before the pastor, the undisputed father of crime. Mansir's gun was already in his hand and he knew that people in the back rows would probably mistake him for a worshipper and could have no way of knowing that he had a gun in his hand.

He wanted the Father to know who was before him, to know the person who was going to kill him and give freedom to many as a result.

Gently, Mansir tapped the Father with his free hand. The Father opened his eyes and looked up. A look of surprise, then fear, creased his thin-featured face. He raised his eyebrows as if to question what Mansir was doing there.

'If you want to pull out, therefore, you must hand back the money in your possession, your flat, your car and the last but not least, your family.' Mansir remembered the Father's words.

The Father's mouth formed into a small, surprised circle as he started to back his hand towards his pocket.

Too late. Still looking into his eyes, Mansir gently squeezed the trigger. The sound exploded into the stillness. The Father staggered back and started to fall. Before he hit the floor, Mansir squeezed the trigger again. The Father's body twitched, then lay still.

Keeping surveillance some metres away, the plainclothes detectives heard the shots and the sound of the mad rush of people to the door of the church.

Women screamed. Children cried. Men shouted. Weak men were trodden on as stronger men charged to the door.

The detectives looked at one another, sprang to their feet and rushed to the scene of whatever it was. One stopped by the door, helping people out. Another rushed inside. A third was about to rush to the telephone when a Land Rover full of policemen stopped by the church. Rifles in hand, the policemen surrounded the church, but could not keep panicking people from running about or getting away in their cars and on their motorcycles.

An old women would have fallen out of the door of the church had it not been for a plain-clothes policeman who helped her.

'Blasphemy,' the old woman mourned. 'To think of a person shooting the pastor! The end of the world has come. It was said so. Blasphemy. God have mercy on my soul! I wish I had never been born to witness such an act of horror!'

The detectives tried in vain to comfort her.

Mansir placed the gun on the passenger seat of his car and pressed his foot flat on the accelerator. The gun was still hot and there was smoke filtering from its barrel. He had managed to escape undetected during the confusion that had followed the shooting.

He was almost scared, perspiring heavily. He couldn't get a firm grip on the steering wheel. He had wanted to finish the Father completely and he had done it now. At least he had helped in confusing the machine of organised crime in Lagos, and in Nigeria as a whole. This was his only offering to his people, the people he used to think cheated him before. How mistaken he was! Or rather, how stupidly he had reacted. If, however, his countrymen were not satisfied with what he offered them, then he would give up his life. He had killed, and it was natural that he would be killed. There was nothing he could do about it.

But as he drove, first increasing speed and then reducing it, he hoped Nigerians would consider the circumstances that led to the killing and spare his life.

He turned left at a T-junction in the direction of the Linivia Island Police compound. Oddly enough, he was experiencing a feeling of relief. After all, he was going to meet his family again.

Susanna, with tears staining her set face, was waiting for him at Inspector Nur's bungalow. When she saw him she embraced him and muttered all the romantic words she knew.

'His wife is very kind and understanding,' she murmured, leading the way to the front door.

'But I can't go inside,' Mansir protested.

'Why not?'

'Nur is a Muslim. He may be strict on the Purdah.'

At this juncture Nur's wife, Lami, opened the front door wide.

'You're welcome,' she said and stood back for them to go into the house. From the way that Lami looked at him, Mansir was sure that his wife has told her everything about him.

Chapter 11

Meanwhile, back at the Black Temple, Inspector Nur, accompanied by armed policemen, marched into the church and muttered as he saw the body of the pastor lying helplessly by the raised pulpit.

'Why, surely it is the pastor!' a policeman exclaimed when they reached the body. 'It was he who reported the Dodge missing.'

Nur nodded and beckoned at the policeman to be attentive. 'According to the man who telephoned us—Mansir, I think he said his name was—the pastor was the chief organiser of the Black Temple, the secret society we are after. I wonder who killed him and why he was killed?' Nur said thoughtfully, going through the pockets of the Father. He found a cheque book and small pistol.

'This,' he said, 'is the seat of the Black Temple. It's my bet that the heroin we were told of—and many other smuggled goods—are in here, locked up securely somewhere. We must also find the list of all the members. It is my suspicion that there are some civil servants who are members, plus a lot of other big men and politicians. Search this place upside down and inside out!'

'Andrews, hurry and call for the ambulance,' Nur said, indicating the body of the Father.

Then, systematically, he started searching the

place—the benches, the pulpit, and even behind the heavy blinds, looking for anything suspicious.

He found nothing. Then he heard a gunshot.

He was about to go into the building when a police officer ran towards him. 'Sir,' the officer gasped, 'we found a room full of bundles of the banned lace material. The room was locked and we had to shoot the lock off!'

Nur half walked and half ran after the man, who led him into a big hall with many doors leading out of it. They went into a room and when he saw the bundles of clothes, Nur just shook his head. Locks on the other doors were burst open. Behind them were hidden jewellery and even cement.

But there was not a single paper containing the list of members. All the drawers were searched. Only a bag of artificially made cowrie shells with the initials 'BT' on each of them was found in one of the drawers. Nur sighed. The matter was getting out of the realms of police work. He must alert the customs and excise department.

For the moment he felt that what he was looking for must be in the church. With the help of other officers, he began to search the place again. Again he found nothing.

Then his eyes fell on the giant crucifix behind the pulpit. He went to the crucifix and inspected it. It did not look suspicious. He tapped it. Some areas sounded hollow and some areas sounded as if they were stuffed with something.

'Get me a sharp, strong knife!' he barked. Within seconds, an officer returned with a sharp, thick knife. Nur inserted the blade of the knife in a crack on the side of the crucifix and pulled at it. The crack opened wider. He pulled harder. A part of the crucifix unexpectedly dropped down to reveal three small, neatly arranged drawers.

In one of them, Nur found what he was looking for. There were three sheets of paper fastened with an office pin. Names and addresses were printed in italics on the papers. The names were divided into sections, viz:—Civil Service, Business, Police Force, and so on.

Nur went to a bench and sat down. Other police officers stared at him, knowing what the paper contained. Nur looked under the section headed Police Force. He was not surprised to see the name: Chief Biodun, Linivia Island Police.

Abruptly, Nur rose and marched to the telephone in the hall. He dialled a number and waited.

'This is the Linivia Island Police...' a voice began.

'Inspector Nur speaking. Is the Chief in?'

'No, sir. He had a headache and went home.'

Nur dialled the Chief's home number and whistled quietly under his breath while he waited for him to answer.

Biodun himself replied. 'Biodun... who is it?'

'Inspector Nur.'

Biodun sucked in his breath. 'I've been expecting you,' he said softly.

'Then you know what I'm ringing about?'

'Yes, I know. It had to happen sooner or later.' He paused. 'In fact, the sooner the better. It's all because of that brainless man, Mansir.'

Mansir, Nur thought. The man who had telephoned them.

'You fall below my expectations, Chief. The Police are entrusted with keeping intact the security of the citizens and here you are, of all people a—. Your sins will catch up with you. The nation needs to get rid of you and your type.'

There was a short silence, then Biodun said, 'My sins have already caught up with me, Nur. Anyway, it will soon all be over. You won't get me alive, Nur.' The Chief paused again. 'Nur? Do you know where I'm talking from? From my bathroom, and I don't think I'm going to get out of it alive. Listen...'

Over the phone Nur heard the sound of a gunshot.

He shook his head and hung up. The Chief had taken the best way out.

He went and told his curious officers what had happened. 'I've gone through the list,' he ended. 'There is no way we can reach most of the men. They are all prominent in the public eye. But we'll try nevertheless.'

A team of customs officials had arrived and all the goods that had been stored in the giant rooms were being loaded into trucks. After about an hour there was nothing left to pack.

Then Nur had another idea.

'Andrews, drive quickly to headquarters and bring a bomb. The only way to cripple this crime machine completely is to wreck the whole place.'

After about an hour, Andrews returned with the time bomb. Together they fixed it and set it to explode in an hour's time. A moment later, the police boarded their vans for Linivia Island Headquarters.

Inspector Nur drove straight home, wondering who the unknown man—Mansir—was. He had helped the police—had it not been for him, the police would not have caught up with the Black Temple. Mansir was a patriot. The nation needed people like him... especially now.

He saw a light blue Peugeot 504 parked by his bungalow. The number plates were not familiar and he wondered who the owner was.

The front door opened and he saw Lami, his wife, walking towards him.

'I've some guests, dear,' she said, opening the door for him. 'They'll interest you. Please be nice to them.'

Nur couldn't wait to tell her what had happened. Without getting out of the car, he said excitedly, 'We have almost finished with the Black Temple...' and briefly told her about his success and about the fate of Biodun, the Chief of Police. Lami listened to him, shocked to the extent of disbelief.

When he had finished, Lami told him about their guests. 'They are in some way or other connected with the Black Temple.'

'Where are they?'

'They are inside.'

'Let's go in, then.'

She clutched his arm. 'Before we do, let me tell you the full story as they told it to me.' And she told him all she knew.

Inspector Nur sat back in the car and folded his arms. For once he was unsure as to what action he should take. The unknown man he had been praising (though he had at one time pondered on the thought that the informer could be an insider laying a trap) was here and the thought of a criminal in his own home made him wonder what to do next.

At this juncture, Mansir, followed by Susanna, walked out of the front door and approached Nur and Lami. Susanna was tugging at Mansir's shirt as if trying to restrain him. In her arms, Shamsiddeen gazed about the new neighbourhood happily.

When Mansir reached Nur, he stretched his arms before him in a gesture that was only too familiar to the police.

'I know I can't be forgiven,' he said. 'I know I can't escape from the hands of the law... that's why I have come. I have killed two people in my life. I regret taking Daudu's life, but as for the Father, I can only shout for joy.'

Susanna cut in. 'It wasn't your fault. There was absolutely nothing you could have done about it. You... you killed Daudu because they had turned you into a human machine. You were bewitched, Mansir, and you know it!'

Nur opened the door of his car and stepped out. He pushed away the outstretched hands of Mansir.

'You certainly took the law into your own hands, Mansir...'

'But if I had not done that you wouldn't have succeeded in seeing the end of the Black Temple.'

'I wish I could be sure that we had seen the last of the Black Temple, Mansir. But really, had you not done what you did, I fear we would not have unmasked any of them. I now have the list of all the members of the Black Temple. But I doubt if we can do much about them because many of them are very powerful men and will find a way of stopping us from taking them to court. Let's go inside now.'

They all went into the bungalow. After they had seated themselves comfortably, Nur spoke. 'There is no way I can help much, you should know that, Mansir. These "mysterious murders" were very sensational and people are still waiting for us to find the murderer.' He paused and leaned forward in his chair. 'But I can make one promise to you—because you have shown a genuine desire to become a decent person again.'

Susanna looked up with tear-stained eyes and face. Mansir turned in his seat.

Nur continued, 'I promise I'll see to it that you spend no more than three years in prison. I'll be the prosecuting officer in the case and I can influence the judge very much in your case.'

There was silence.

Susanna patted Mansir's hand gently. 'I'll wait for you, Mansir,' she sobbed. 'I'll take care of the restaurant. Then when you come out we'll really be in... in big business.'

Mansir caressed her and thanked the Inspector for his promise. For the first time since Daudu's death, he felt his conscience clearing once again and the feeling of guilt began to ebb away.

To add weight to his promise, Nur added 'Society needs no one more than a reformed man, Mansir.'

At exactly that moment, there was a muffled boom as the time bomb at the Amoto People's Church exploded, putting an end to the building that had once hidden the Black Temple.